Mills & Boon
Best Seller Romance

A chance to read and collect some of the best-loved novels
from Mills & Boon—the world's largest publisher of
romantic fiction.

Every month, six titles by favourite Mills & Boon authors
will be re-published in the *Best Seller Romance* series.

A list of other titles in the *Best Seller Romance* series
can be found at the end of this book.

Flora Kidd

NIGHT OF THE
YELLOW MOON

MILLS & BOON LIMITED

LONDON·TORONTO

First published 1977
Australian copyright 1983
Philippine copyright 1978
This edition 1983

© Flora Kidd 1977

ISBN 0 263 74490 6

Set in Linotype Granjon 10 on 12 pt.
02–1183

Made and printed in Great Britain by
Richard Clay (The Chaucer Press) Ltd,
Bungay, Suffolk

CHAPTER ONE

'Looks like your aunt and uncle have a visitor,' said Brian Collins as he brought his rather battered green sports car to a sudden screeching stop behind a gleaming white Jaguar car which was parked at the front entrance of the Tudor-styled creeper-covered cottage.

'Oh, it's probably someone from the University. Or perhaps one of Uncle Roy's ex-students. I think he said one of them was in the district and might drop in this week-end,' replied Delia, picking up her tennis racket and string bag of balls. 'Thanks for the lift, Brian, and for the games.'

'Won't we see you later?' asked Sue Martin, who was sitting in the front of the car with Brian. 'We're all going into Southleigh this evening. There's a new discothèque opened on the promenade. I believe it's fabulous. Like to come with us?'

Standing outside the car, Delia looked from Sue to Brian and back to Sue again. By 'we' Sue meant herself and Brian and two other young couples belonging to the tennis club, all local people whom Delia had known on and off during the years she had been coming to stay for week-ends and holidays with Marsha and Roy. If she went with them this evening she would be the 'odd girl out', something which she was often and something which she was beginning to dislike being.

'Thanks for the invite,' she said lightly with her brightest smile and a show of nonchalance. 'I think I'd better stay at home and help entertain the visitor.'

'Oh, come on, Delia,' said Sue. 'He's probably some middle-aged general practitioner escaped for the week-end from his patients. He's probably a frightful bore, married and with two or three kids.'

'I'll take a chance on that,' retorted Delia, laughing. 'See you next month. I'll be down for my holidays.'

The little car went off with a roar. Still smiling, Delia waited until it had gone through the gateway into the narrow lane, then, her smile fading, she turned and walked slowly to the front door, swinging her tennis racket idly, a slim young woman in a crisp short-skirted tennis dress, her smooth dark brown hair shining under the rays of the sun.

In the small hallway of the cottage horse-brasses glinted on dark wood and antique copper jugs were crammed full of greenery and sweet-smelling summer flowers. Hearing her aunt's clear and rather strident voice coming from the direction of the lounge, Delia supposed she had better look into the room to show she was back and to be introduced to the visitor. Marsha and Roy often had week-end guests, usually professors or lecturers from the nearby University where both of them worked, Roy as a professor of physiology in the Faculty of Medicine and Marsha as a lecturer in sociology in the Social Science department.

It sounded as if Marsha was working hard to make an impression, thought Delia with an impish grin which put dimples in her soft pink cheeks and a glint of mischief into her greyish-green eyes, so it wasn't hard to guess that the visitor was a man. She pushed open the panelled oak door further, looked into the room. Her heart seemed to miss a beat, she stood stock still and stared, looked at him and loved.

He was lounging against the back of the chintz-covered settee and he was casually dressed in dark blue pants and a dark blue shirt which was open at the neck and half way down the front. His face was lean and clean-shaven, tanned to an even golden brown. The forehead was high and broad, the cheekbones prominent, the nose high-bridged, long and straight, the jaw square and clean-cut. All were framed by thick curly brown hair, much fairer than her own, which glinted here and there with golden flecks in the sunlight shafting through the window behind him.

Marsha was sitting opposite to him on the other settee, leaning forward and talking enthusiastically. Roy was sitting in his favourite wing chair listening and nodding indulgently as his wife talked. The guest wasn't listening, Delia could tell by the expression of boredom on his handsome face, and he was looking down at the contents of the glass he was holding in one hand.

Then Marsha asked him a question. There was a brief silence. The guest looked up. His eyes glimmered brilliantly blue between thick bronze-coloured lashes under finely marked eyebrows. Delia held her breath to stop herself from bursting out laughing at his predicament, for it was obvious to her that he hadn't the slightest idea what the question was about.

He was disconcerted for a moment only. A smile curved his well-shaped mouth and softened the angularity of his lean face and Delia felt suddenly dizzy.

'Naturally I agree with you, Mrs Halton,' he drawled, his voice deep and soft. 'The jungle isn't the place for a woman who is used to all the amenities of your way of life.'

Roy Halton laughed out loud and clapped his knee with his hand.

'Dammit, Edmund, I always used to think you'd chosen the wrong profession. You should have been a diplomat, not a doctor,' he exclaimed.

Marsha continued to talk lightly, provocatively. The man facing her raised the glass in his hand to his mouth and drained it, as Delia moved forward. Her slight movement drew his attention as he lowered the glass. He turned his head and looked straight at her. For Delia it was a moment out of time, a breathless fateful moment as their glances met and locked. Drawn towards him by a strange magnetism, she advanced into the room.

'Ah, here you are at last, love,' Roy said, rising to his feet. The guest unfolded his lean length from the settee and stood up politely. Roy introduced them.

'I'm pleased to meet you, Dr Talbot,' Delia said stiltedly, overwhelmed by a sudden unaccountable shyness, and went to sit by Marsha.

'Edmund was one of the star students of my physiology class some years ago,' Roy was explaining.

'You'll have another drink, Edmund?' asked Marsha, rising to her feet and going over to take his empty glass from his hand. Tall, dark-haired and shapely, she was wearing a close-fitting dress of yellow and black spotted material which gave the effect of shimmering leopardskin. She returned with a full, ice-clinking glass, her figure swaying voluptuously as she teetered on her high heels. Sitting down beside Edmund Talbot, she offered him the drink, leaning forward towards him so that the deep plunging neckline of her dress sagged away from her breasts leaving very little to anyone's imagination.

Delia scowled, recognising Marsha's tactics only too well. It wasn't the first time she had seen her aunt making up to a man other than her husband, especially a man younger than herself. Attractive and dynamic in her middle age, Marsha was finding life with Roy, who was almost twenty years her senior and close to retiring age, just a little dull and was trying to enliven it with the occasional extra-marital affair. There was no doubt that she considered Edmund Talbot with his graceful body, curly hair and deep blue eyes a suitable partner for such an affair.

'Is it safe to go swimming from the beach here?' Edmund asked suddenly and quite irrelevantly in the middle of a discussion about tropical diseases.

'Of course it is,' said Marsha, smiling. 'Do you like to swim, Edmund?'

'Very much, especially in the sea. Would you mind if I went swimming now?'

'Not at all, not at all.' Roy was enthusiastic. 'Please make yourself at home while you're here. Delia will show you the way to the beach. It isn't far, just down the lane.'

'You'll want to change into your swimming things, I expect,' said Marsha, rising to her feet again. 'Come with me and I'll show you to the room where I've put your overnight bag. Delia will meet you at the front door when you're ready.'

Edmund went with Marsha from the room and after a few words with Roy Delia also went upstairs to change into her bikini in the small room with the sloping ceiling which she always considered as hers. When she left it a few minutes later to go downstairs she could hear the murmur of her aunt's voice coming from the guest room along the landing and she frowned. Surely it wasn't necessary for Marsha to go right into the room with the guest?

She waited almost twenty minutes for Edmund to appear and they walked together down the lane between the high hedges of sweet-smelling laurel, where swallows swooped, to the small cove rimmed with pale yellow sand and backed by crumbling chalk-white cliffs which were topped by green grass.

Edmund dropped his towel to the sand, removed his trousers and shirt without any thought for anyone who might be watching and sped into the water which stretched like flat blue silk into a hazy blue distance where a few sail boats drifted about with their sails flopping idly. A little piqued at being left behind, Delia followed him. She could see he was a highly competent swimmer and she kept up with him to show him she was his equal, but when he continued to ignore her she left the water and went to sit on the sand and watch him.

After a while he came out and flung himself down on the beach a little in front of her.

'That's better,' he said, pushing his wet hair back. 'Your aunt pours a strong drink and I'm not used to alcohol. For a while I felt quite disorientated back there in the house.' He laughed with a touch of self-mockery, rolled over on to his stomach, rested his chin on his folded arms and looked up at her. 'So you're Frank Fenwick's daughter,' he drawled. 'I find it hard to believe.'

'Why?' she exclaimed, opening her eyes wide.

'I never thought of him as being married, let alone having any children,' he replied.

'Did you ever meet him?' she challenged.

'Yes, I attended a series of lectures he gave about ten years ago on the need for us to protect the primitive peoples of the world, the tribes which live in inaccessible places in Indonesia and South America. It was those talks of his which inspired me to specialise in tropical medicine once I'd qualified as a doctor so that I could go and work with such people.'

'Have you been yet to see any of them?' she asked, excited by the fact that he had known her father about whom she knew so little.

'Yes, I'm just back from Africa where I've been working for an international health organisation.'

'When will you go again?'

'When someone asks me to go or when the itch to go comes. Right now all I want to do is have a good time living it up in London.' He gave her another underbrowed glance. 'Preferably with an attractive woman for company. Would you be interested?'

Without waiting for a reply to his offhand question he rolled over on to his back. The beach was almost deserted at this time of day because the afternoon swimmers and sunbathers had gone home for tea. But the sun was still warm and the sky still hazy with heat. The only sounds were the lapping of water and the occasional cackle of a seagull.

Delia's cheeks tingled with the blood which had rushed to them at his casual suggestion that she could be the attractive woman who could keep him company in London. She piled up a little heap of sand with one hand, wondering how she should answer him. She wanted to be that woman, very much so, but, shy and inexperienced in the ways of young men, she didn't want to appear too eager to accept his invitation.

'Do you find Aunt Marsha attractive?' she asked. Out of the corner of her eyes she studied his bare torso. Grains of sand and drops of water, glinting like diamonds in the sunlight, clung to the criss-cross of brown hairs on his chest. Otherwise he was unadorned. There was no chain with a medallion around his neck, no beads, and the clean spare lines of his body and limbs made an appeal to her senses which was new and slightly shocking.

'She's remarkably well preserved for her age,' he replied diplomatically.

'She's almost forty-one,' she said, determined to make him see Aunt Marsha for what she was.

'Ten years older than I am,' he murmured. 'How old are you?'

'Twenty-one.'

'Thank heavens for that,' he said mockingly. 'I was beginning to think that perhaps you were still at school.'

'Perhaps you prefer older women,' she jibed, knowing she was treading on dangerous ground yet wanting to find out somehow what had happened when Marsha had shown him to his room.

'I admit there are times when experience in how to please can make up for lack of youth in a woman,' he retorted, his voice shaking a little with laughter as if he was finding the whole conversation highly amusing.

'Did Aunt Marsha please you when she showed you to your room?' she queried. 'I heard her talking to you in there.'

He didn't react at once, but when he did it was with a suddenness which caught her offguard. Sitting up in one smoothe lithe movement, he turned on her, grasped her face with lean fingers and forced it round so he could see it. His eyes were a hard metallic blue and there was a nasty curve to his mouth.

'Just what are you getting at?' he drawled menacingly.

Although her heart was fluttering crazily Delia managed to return his gaze and to speak coolly.

'She likes you. I expect she'd like to have an affair with you. Oh, you're not the first man younger than she is that she's made up to. I've seen her do it before. She made your drinks too strong. She hoped you'd be tight and a little careless so that you wouldn't mind what happened when she showed you to your room ...'

'That's enough.' He didn't raise his voice, but the steely

tone of it made her stop. He was so close to her that she felt his breath feather across her mouth like a caress. His fingers relaxed, slid across her cheek and wound in a damp tress of her hair which spiralled over her shoulder. 'Nothing happened when she showed me to my room,' he continued softly. 'I'm not exactly a callow youth unused to the ways of women and unable to fend off a seductress when I come across one. But you'd better keep that imagination of yours under control before it gets you into trouble, you jealous little cat.'

'I'm not jealous,' she protested, trying to move away from him, only to find that his grasp on her hair was tight.

'If you're not jealous why all the fuss about Marsha and me?' he taunted.

'I . . . I . . . don't like to see her behaving the way she did this afternoon in front of Roy. He's so good and kind to her,' she mumbled desperately.

'Are you sure that's the reason?' he challenged. 'Wouldn't it be more true to say you can't bear the thought of her and me being together because you want to be with me yourself?'

'No, it wouldn't. Oh, how conceited you are to suggest that!' she raged, furious because he had discovered a truth she had been unwilling to acknowledge about herself. Then realising he was laughing at her she tried to slap him, missed, tried to pull away and cried out when her caught hair tugged at her scalp. 'Ah, let me go, please let me go!'

'Now that I've caught you I don't want to, little mermaid,' he whispered. 'Mmm, you smell of the sea and some other perfume. I think it's sandalwood.'

'And you smell of rum,' she accused, but he only laughed at her and with his lips close to her cheek murmured,

'That could be, but I'm finding you far more intoxicating than Marsha's drinks.'

His lips touched her cheek near the corner of her mouth

and then moved on to cover her lips in a ruthless kiss. Vainly Delia twisted her head from side to side in an effort to break free, but her efforts only increased his desire to keep hold of her. His hand tightened on the back of her neck so that she couldn't move her head at all. He pushed her backwards until she was lying against the sand and she could feel its grains scratching against her bare skin as his mouth continued to take its toll of hers and his hard muscular body crushed the softness of her breasts which were barely covered by the bodice of her bikini.

The stifling warmth of his lips, the rubbing of his damp bare skin against hers sent her senses spinning. She had no idea of time or place. She knew only the quick urgent demand of his body and felt the slow rising of a desire within herself to satisfy his demand totally and without restraint.

Her lips softened and opened. Her hands lifted to the damp tangle of his hair and she thrust her fingers through it. She touched his bare shoulders experimentally and finding there was a sensuous pleasure in the feel of his skin against her palms she experimented more and stroked downwards over his taut bare back.

He relaxed in a sigh against her. The touch of his mouth became tender and exploratory, trailing down from her mouth to her throat to press against the hollow between her breasts. She felt his curls brush against her chin and a little shiver of ecstasy tingled through her.

'You're pretty,' he said softly, raising his head to look into her eyes. 'And you're sweet and tender like a new shoot in spring. And you have green eyes. Why should anyone want Marsha when you're around? Am I going to see more of you? Will you come up to London to meet me there?'

Joy exploded within her because this handsome, god-like

person had been dropped into her life and actually wanted to see her again because he liked her.

'I work in London and live there,' she replied, daring to show her liking for him by tracing the outline of his mouth with one finger tip.

'That's even better. We'll be able to see each other every day. Where do you work?'

'At the Multiple Publishing Company. I'm in the editorial department of *Geography Illustrated*.'

'Following in your father's footsteps?' he jeered gently.

'I'd like to, one day, but I'm still learning how to write.'

'Where do you live?'

'I share a flat with another girl in Kensington.'

'Is that far from Knightsbridge?'

'No, not really. Why?'

'A friend of mine, Pete Manson, has lent me his flat there for six weeks while he's on holiday in the Mediterranean, and I wondered how near to each other we'd be. I'm glad it isn't far. Is Marsha your only relative?'

'Yes. She's my mother's younger sister. My mother died when I was twelve. Daddy was away a lot, so he sent me to a boarding school near here and I always came to Marsha and Roy for holidays. You must know what happened to Daddy. He was killed in a helicopter crash in Ethiopia about five years ago.'

'Yes, I read about it.'

'Do you have any family?' she asked shyly.

'My father died a few years ago too,' he replied with a touch of reserve in his manner. 'My mother is married to someone else now and lives in Italy.'

'No brothers or sisters?'

'No. Only dozens of uncles, aunts and cousins. But you don't have to worry about them. You're not likely to meet any of them,' he said, kissing the tip of her nose. 'Can I drive you back to London tomorrow, leaving here as soon as we can? I want you all to myself far away from your aunt's curious eyes. She's standing at an upstairs bedroom window of the cottage watching us through binoculars just now.'

'Oh no!' Delia sat up abruptly and scrambled to her feet, and shading her eyes with her hand stared in the direction of the cottage. Sure enough Marsha was at a window holding Roy's powerful binoculars to her eyes.

Later that night when Delia, still dazed with love, was about to get into bed Marsha came into her room.

'You seem to be getting on very well with Edmund Talbot,' she said, going straight to the point in her usual forthright manner. 'I hope you're not going to take his sudden interest in you seriously.'

'Shouldn't I?' Delia countered as she settled into bed. Marsha came to stand beside the bed and look down at her. With her dark brown hair unwound and straggling on her shoulders, without make-up, she looked tired and a little haggard.

'Listen, darling,' she said earnestly, sitting down on the edge of the bed. 'Since your mother died I've tried hard to take her place in your life and guide you as I think she would have liked you to be guided, but perhaps I haven't been as frank on some subjects as I should have been.'

'If you mean you haven't told me the facts of life,' Delia said with a gurgle of laughter, 'you're quite right, you haven't. But it's all right, Aunty, I know them and I can take care of myself and have done up till now.'

'I know, darling,' said Marsha with a sigh. 'But you're still very innocent when it comes to people and you could make an awful mistake with this doctor. He isn't what he seems. Under that surface warmth and charm he's a cool, tough customer.'

'You're only saying that because you weren't able to make an impression on him,' Delia accused, shakily, not wanting to hear any defamation of Edmund. 'But just because you failed to seduce him it doesn't mean that there's anything wrong with him.'

'I'm sure I don't know what you're talking about,' retorted Marsha icily, her grey eyes flashing angrily. 'I'm trying to point out to you that Edmund is the type who loves and leaves because his work is more important to him than any woman. So you want to be careful what you do when you're with him. And he's also a bit of a hippy—likes to go off into the jungle and live with primitive tribes. Says he prefers the simple life with minimum of possessions. Now you don't want to become involved with anyone like that, do you?'

'I don't care what he is or what he does,' replied Delia dreamily. 'I like him, and tomorrow I'm going to London with him and we're going to see each other every day.'

Marsha stood up suddenly and swept across the room to the door. There she turned and glared back at Delia rather viciously.

'Then you're a fool, just like your mother was, and one day you'll be sorry you didn't listen to me, but when that time comes you needn't come running to me for help.'

Convinced that her aunt's warnings had been prompted by spite because Edmund had rejected her advances to him, Delia ignored them and once back in London spent all her spare time during the following week with Edmund so that by Friday night she found herself admitting to him that she was in love with him.

'Then you'll stay the night, here, with me,' he whispered as they sat side by side on the settee in Peter Manson's luxuriously furnished apartment.

'I ... I ... can't,' replied Delia, even though she longed to give in to his request with every fibre of her body.

'Why not?' he countered, kissing her neck just below her ear, at the same time sliding his fingers under the edge of her blouse opening to curl his fingers over her breast.

'S-something inside won't let me,' she quavered.

'Then all your talk about loving me is a lie,' he retorted, springing to his feet suddenly and walking over to the window to look out at the lights of the city which were just beginning to glimmer in the late summer dusk.

'Oh, it isn't, it isn't! I do love you,' she protested. 'But I can't stay with you. I can't live with you unless ... unless ...'

'Unless there's a ring on your finger and you have the right to use my surname, is that it?' he interrupted her, swinging round to look at her, and she could only nod. 'And I'd thought you were different,' he added softly yet stingingly.

Realising she had disappointed him, unable to do as he had asked because she was suddenly unsure of how he felt about her, Delia stood up, fastened her blouse properly and pushed it into the waistband of her ssirt. She went across to the chair where she had thrown her suit jacket when she had entered the room. Picking the jacket up, she pulled it on without bothering to fasten it.

'If ... if ... you love me as I love you you'd ask me to marry you first,' she muttered miserably, and grabbing her handbag she slung the strap over her shoulder and made rather blindly for the door.

He was there before her, leaning against it, long and lean with a thin clever face topped by curling brown hair and lit by blue eyes which could dance with gentle mockery or look through you coldly.

'Where are you going?' he asked quietly.

'I don't know!' she cried out wildly, not wanting to go anywhere where he wouldn't be.

He stepped towards her. His hands curved about her cheeks. For a moment he studied her face and there was no laughter dancing in his eyes, no coldness either, only a dark unnerving sadness. Then he smiled, a half-tender, half-challenging smile.

'All right, we'll do it your way, mermaid. We'll get married as soon as it can be arranged quietly with the least fuss possible, because I want you to live with me while I'm here.' And quite suddenly they were clinging to each other like two lonely children lost in the dark. 'Oh, Delia,' Edmund half groaned and half laughed against her hair. 'The smell of you, the feel of you has sent me out of my mind and I don't know what I'm doing any more. You've come between me and sanity.'

It was a strange remark for him to make, but she didn't question it. She was too happy. So they were married quietly and unobtrusively and she went to live with him at Peter's flat while they searched for a flat of their own. And they were happy those first two weeks, at least Delia was, ecstatically happy, as Edmund proved to be the sort of lover she had always imagined she would like to have, demanding yet considerate of her desires and helping her to fulfil them.

On the day before Peter Manson was due to return from his holidays Edmund went to Oxford to a meeting of some organisation which was concerned with the welfare of primitive tribes in various countries in the world. Returning to the Knightsbridge flat after work, Delia began to pack their belongings ready for moving out. She was just finishing packing her own clothes when she heard someone enter the flat. Thinking it was Edmund, she hurried out into the living room and exclaimed with surprise when she saw a tall dark-haired, good-looking man about the same age as Edmund standing there looking through the mail which had come and which was stacked neatly on the sideboard.

He was equally surprised to see her, and when she explained quickly who she was and why she was there his mouth gaped in spontaneous surprise.

'Edmund married?' he exclaimed. 'Oh, no! I can't believe that. You're pulling my leg.' His dark eyes twinkled as he recovered from the surprise and he stroked his dark moustache with his fingers. 'Come on, now, no need to be coy with me. I know Edmund too well. He's always said he'd never get married. You don't need to cover up with a tale like that. I'm not offended because you and he are living together in my flat. I expected something like this to happen.'

'But we're not . . .' she began to object. Then realising how silly it would sound to say that she and Edmund weren't living together when they were, she flung out her left hand. The plain gold ring on her third finger glinted. 'There. Does that convince you?' she challenged.

He looked suitably taken aback. His hand went to his neatly-styled dark hair and smoothed it unnecessarily and he stared at her with puzzled eyes.

'Good God,' he said in a hushed voice, and sat down suddenly in an armchair. 'Excuse me, but I'm really shaken by this and don't seem to be able to take it in. Edmund has always been such a loner, dedicated to tropical medicine. How long have you known him?'

'Six weeks,' she muttered, and it didn't sound long enough.

'Oh, my God!' Peter Manson sprang to his feet and digging his hands in the trouser pockets of his elegant three-piece grey lounge suit began to pace up and down the room. 'I wouldn't be at all surprised if you know nothing about him,' he accused, stopping abruptly in front of her, his hazel eyes boring down into hers.

'I know all that matters,' she retorted, lifting her chin. 'I know how old he is and what he likes doing. What more do I need to know? I love him, and that's all that matters.'

Peter's eyes narrowed thoughtfully and he smiled slightly, tolerantly.

'A romantic, eh?' he remarked. 'So he hasn't told you,' he added tantalisingly as he began to pace again, and she took the bait.

'Told me what?' she asked, imagining rather wildly that Edmund might have committed bigamy in marrying her and the fact that he might have had a wife already had been the reason of his hesitation about marrying.

'He hasn't told you that he inherited a fortune when his father died a few years ago?' Peter flung at her over his shoulder on his third time round the room.

'Well, I know he isn't short of money, even though he doesn't seem to own anything much apart from a Jaguar sports car and a few clothes,' she replied.

'Not short of money, ha!' Peter's laughter was mocking as he came to stand before her again. 'He's worth several hundred thousands of pounds, all made from toffee. Now you're not going to tell me you've never heard of Talbot's Toffees,' he added scornfully.

She had of course heard of them and had often bought them, but she had never connected them with Edmund.

'Edmund doesn't seem like a toffee maker,' she said rather foolishly.

'He isn't, and has nothing to do with the business, which is now owned entirely by some cousin or other. He would never have anything to do with it, much to his father's disappointment,' said Peter. 'No, Edmund is the odd one out in his family. He always wanted to be a doctor and to help people less fortunate than himself. He even tried to persuade his father to leave the money to a philanthropic organisation instead of to himself. But Matthew Talbot refused and said he would leave his money to his own flesh and blood and that after he was dead Edmund could do what the hell he liked with it. Edmund has too, using it to finance his studies in tropical medicine at Oxford and his expeditions to various jungles.' Peter paused and frowned. 'And that's something else you've got to consider. What are you going to do when he goes off to live in some isolated, malaria-infested swamp in Africa or Brazil?'

'I'll go with him,' Delia retorted promptly, and he gave her a pitying glance.

'I doubt it, because if I know Edmund as well as I think I do he won't take you. He believes in the old adage that he travels fastest who travels alone.'

'You were mistaken about him once, so you could be mistaken about him again,' she replied. 'You didn't think he would marry.'

'That's why I'm worried about you,' he said with a sigh. 'Oh, I can see why he likes you and wants your company while he's here in England, but he won't always be here and he isn't the domesticated type.'

She must have looked very distressed because he passed a hand over his face and shook his head apologetically.

'I'm sorry, Delia, I'm saying all the wrong things. I should be congratulating you, wishing you all the best, and I do quite sincerely. I hope you believe that.'

She tried to believe him, but she was disturbed. Then Edmund returned from Oxford and the doubts Peter had raised in her mind were obliterated. They moved into their own flat and she settled down to the delights of living and loving with Edmund.

For three months they lived contentedly. Delia continued to work for the magazine and Edmund commuted daily between London and Oxford where he was engaged in some research to do with tropical diseases. During that time she learned that though Edmund liked to live simply he wasn't above spending money extravagantly on her. She also learned that he was very sensitive on the subject of his inherited wealth and had donated large amounts of it to charities. When she asked him why he hadn't told her of his association with Talbot's Toffees, he said coolly,

'I didn't want you to get any ideas about marrying me for my money. I nearly got caught like that once.'

'You mean you nearly married someone before you met me?' she asked in surprise.

'Yes.' His mouth twisted cynically. 'I was almost at the point of making vows at the altar when I found out it was my inheritance she was interested in and not me.'

'Oh, how awful!' she gasped, putting her arms round him to comfort him.

'It was very disillusioning,' he murmured.

'Were you in love with her?' she asked, face hidden against the pulsating warmth of his neck.

'Not as much as I am with you,' he replied diplomatically, curving his hands about her head to hold it away from him so that he could kiss her.

Then one day he came home to tell he had been asked to serve on a Red Cross relief team being sent to an area in Indonesia which had been devastated by an earthquake and where it was believed that thousands of primitive people were suffering from disease and hunger.

'Can I come with you?' asked Delia.

'No.'

'Why not?'

'Obvious reasons. Only doctors, nurses and social workers can go. Anyway, I wouldn't want you to come out there. I'd feel happier knowing you're here safe and comfortable ... waiting for me to come back.'

It hurt to be left behind, but she accepted it. Peter helped by calling on her often and sometimes taking her out to a theatre or to dinner because, he said, Edmund had asked him to keep an eye on her.

Edmund was away much longer than she expected, almost seven months. She was overjoyed when he returned at last, thin and tough as tarred rope, with hardly any luggage and his clothes almost in rags. He shrugged off his adventures with a careless 'Oh, it was nothing much,' and seemed intent on enjoying himself with her. He went personally to see her boss, Ben Davies, and asked that she might be allowed at least two weeks'-holiday so that she could be with him all the time.

He stayed in England for nearly six weeks. Then he was asked to go with another relief team to Central America where another earthquake had wreaked destruction in a jungle area. Again Delia pleaded to go with him and again he refused to take her, with the result they had their first serious quarrel, and although they both tried to make it up there was a definite coolness in his attitude to her when he left.

While he was away Delia worried incessantly in case he didn't come back to her. Once again Peter 'kept an eye' on her and she was grateful for his concern, but she missed Edmund terribly. Even so she was unprepared for his return less than a month after he had left, one day in September.

It was Sunday. Peter called and suggested they drove

down to the coast for a change. They returned to hers and Edmund's flat in the early evening. Peter went up to the flat with her as he often did and Delia offered him a drink, which she usually did when he escorted her home.

They were sitting on the settee in the twilight when Peter turned to her suddenly and said,

'It's at times like this that I wish you weren't married to Edmund.'

She wasn't surprised by the statement. For some time she had been noticing that he was more attentive, had called on her more often and issued more invitations, and it had occurred to her that she should start refusing to go out with him. She shouldn't be sitting here with him close on the settee.

About to move away, she found her hand caught in his, and looked at him enquiringly.

'You realise I've done the unforgivable, darling,' he murmured. 'I've fallen in love with my best friend's wife and I'm going to take advantage of his absence from home. I can't keep my distance any longer.'

'No, Peter, no!' she whispered, desperately putting her hands against his shoulders to push him away as he moved in on her, but he wouldn't be denied. His arms went round her and his mouth sought hers. She turned her head quickly and the kiss fell somewhere on her hair, but she didn't really feel it because she was staring in shocked surprise over his shoulder. It seemed to her that someone was standing in the doorway which led into the narrow hallway of the flat, a dim shadowy figure in the fast-deepening gloom; a familiar figure. Was it really Edmund? Or was it a figment of her imagination?

The figure vanished when she gasped. Hearing her gasp, Peter withdrew slightly.

'Sorry, Delia, I got carried away,' he said, stroking a strand of her hair back from her face. 'You're so lovely and so sad, in need of comfort. Won't you let me stay and comfort you?'

'No, please, Peter, don't say things like that, don't even think them. If you do I shan't be able to see you any more or go anywhere with you. Please go now,' she whispered, sending another glance to the doorway. The shadowy figure hadn't reappeared.

To her relief Peter stood up.

'All right, I'll go,' he said. 'But I'll be back to see you again, you can be sure of that. After all, didn't someone say once all's fair in love and war? And I'm in love with you and I want you.'

'Oh, Peter, it isn't any use. You're wasting your time,' she said. 'I'm married . . .'

'That's a situation which can soon be remedied, as you should know,' he retorted, turning towards her as they stood by the front door of the flat. 'Yours isn't much of a marriage. Edmund is hardly ever here.'

'Please, Peter, stop! I don't want to hear any more,' she cried in a low voice in case the figure she had seen wasn't a figment of her imagination, in case Edmund was somewhere in the flat and could hear what was being said. 'Will you go now?' She opened the door. He smiled down at her, his bright self-confident smile.

'You're a fool, Delia, to stay faithful to him, do you know that? I doubt very much if he's faithful to you.'

'Goodnight, Peter, and thank you for taking me to the sea today,' she said woodenly, and closed the door after him. But the doubt he had expressed clanged about in her mind as she hurried down the hallway, past the living room to the bedroom. The door was closed. She opened it slowly. The room was shadowy within, lit only from the glow of the street lamps. Her heart leapt and began to pound against her ribs when she saw that there was a figure standing by the window.

'Edmund?' she asked, and clicked on the light switch by the door. At once the two bedside lamps went on, making pools of golden light on the ceiling and dispersing the shadows in the room. The figure by the window turned to look at her. An oblique shaft of light from a lamp revealed that he was wearing a short dressing gown of blue silk open to the waist where it was belted. The light burnished the skin of his chest and his bare legs, giving the deep suntan a coppery hue. In the shadowed eye sockets his eyes seemed to burn like blue flames as they regarded her.

But he didn't move towards her and knowing what he had just seen in the living room and how it must have looked to him, she stood hesitantly by the door instead of rushing up to him to fling her arms about him and kiss him welcome.

'When did you get back?' she asked at last, her voice hurried and breathless. She felt guilty because she hadn't been at home when he arrived.

'About an hour ago, I think,' he replied coolly. 'I was in the bathroom getting rid of a month's growth of beard and soaking out all the sweat and filth of the place where I've been and didn't hear you come back. I didn't know you were in until I heard Pete's voice as I left the bathroom.'

'I ... I'm sorry I wasn't home,' Delia said nervously, advancing into the room. 'I wasn't expecting you today, that's why I went out. Peter and I drove down to the sea. It was such a lovely day and ...'

'Has he gone now?' he interrupted harshly. 'Or does he usually stay the night after you and he have been out together?'

She gasped at the implication and moved forward urgently, going right up to him. He looked thin and tired, she noticed, but the expression in his eyes frightened her. They smouldered with barely controlled anger.

'He's gone,' she said breathlessly, her hands going out to rest on his arms as if by touching him she could impress him with the truth. 'Oh, Edmund, don't look like that! I can explain about what you saw just now. It wasn't what you're thinking. It's never happened before. It meant nothing . . .'

'How am I to know that?' he interrupted her again. 'How the hell am I to know what you're doing when I'm away?'

Appalled by his answer and not knowing how to deal with this furious different Edmund who seemed to have no relation to the tender loving companion of the first months of their marriage, Delia stepped back from him.

'I don't do anything,' she whispered forlornly. 'I go to work and I come back here to wait for you. Oh, Edmund, if you knew how lonely I've been without you !'

'Lonely?' he queried with an ironic lift of his eyebrows. 'You expect me to believe that after what I saw happening in the living room, after you've told me you've been out all day with Peter . . .'

'Well, you told him to keep an eye on me while you were away,' she defended herself.

'There's a hell of a lot of difference between keeping an eye on someone and moving in to take possession,' he replied with a dry bitterness.

'He hasn't moved in and taken possession. Oh, how can you say that? How can you believe that?' she flared suddenly, caught in a storm of helpless anger because instead of being in each other's arms trying to make up for all the weeks they had been apart they were quarrelling. 'You say you don't know what I do while you're away. Well, I could say the same. How am I to know what you do when you're thousands of miles away, when I don't even know if you're ... you're still alive...' Her voice shook a little and she drew a deep breath to steady it. 'For all I know you could have a woman in each of the four corners of the earth ...'

It was the wrong thing to say, she could see that as soon as the words were out of her mouth. It had the effect of petrol thrown on a smouldering fire. Edmund blazed suddenly and she stepped back—too late because, moving with that swiftness which always surprised her, he scooped her up in his arms and carried her over to the bed. He dropped her on to the soft damask cover, and alarmed by the swift savagery of his action she tried to roll away from him, but he was too quick for her.

His hands gripped the sides of her head so cruelly that she was unable to twist it and avoid his mouth which came down on hers in a brutal insolent kiss which gave her no chance to respond. The weight of his body pinned her down relentlessly so that she couldn't move. Frightened by the fury which she had unwittingly aroused, she tried to struggle and push him off, but her struggles only seemed to inflame him more and for the first time in their relationship there was no tenderness or gentleness in his possession of her, no consideration of her desires.

When it was over and he released her he leaned over her to whisper tautly,

'That was just to make sure you know who's in possession here—me, your husband. When I come back I hope you'll be a little more loving and welcoming.'

He swung off the bed, pulled on his dressing gown and went from the room, closing the door quietly. After a while Delia rose from the bed and went along to the bathroom to bathe her face, which was blotched with crying. Returning to the bedroom, she ignored the dress and underwear he had stripped from her and dressed in light woollen slacks and a coloured tunic top. She was sitting in front of the dressing table combing her hair and crying silently inside herself because she seemed to have lost the Edmund she loved and had in his place a violent punishing stranger, when he returned to the room carrying, of all things, a cup of tea.

He set the cup and saucer in front of her on the dressing table and looked down at her. She refused to return his glance and stared woodenly at the cup of tea. He squatted down beside her and taking her chin in one hand turned her face so he could see it and so that she had to look at him. His eyes darkened with compassion and the line of his mouth softened. Releasing her chin, he touched her swollen mouth with gentle fingers.

'I'm sorry,' he said softly.

But Delia was still too upset, too overwrought by what had happened to behave sensibly. She started back from him and sprang to her feet, overturning the stool in her attempt to escape from him.

'Don't touch me, don't touch me!' she hurled the words at him and he straightened up, folded his arms across his chest tightly as if it was the only way he could prevent himself from touching her.

'I didn't mean to hurt you,' he said, and his voice was as usual deep and soft. He raised a hand and rubbed at his forehead. 'I don't know what happened,' he added. 'I suppose I was disappointed when I arrived here and you were out. I'd managed to come home sooner than expected because I wanted to be with you. I thought it would be a pleasant surprise.' He took a sharp shuddering breath and added more harshly, 'Oh God, Delia, stop looking at me as if I'm some sort of monster! I didn't mean to hurt you. I've said I'm sorry. What else do I have to say or do to make you believe me?'

He stepped towards her again and she stepped backwards. All she could think was that he wasn't the man she had fallen in love with and had expected to come back to her.

'You can't say or do anything,' she cried. 'Oh, why did you have to come back today? Why did you have to spoil everything by coming back when you weren't expected?' She saw him stiffen. His face went pale and she realised that what she had said could be misconstrued. Her hands went to her face. 'Oh, that's not what I mean. Oh, I can't bear it any longer! What am I going to do?'

She rushed over to the wardrobe, snatched a coat from a hanger and pulled it on. Her one aim was to get out of the flat, to be alone for a few minutes to sort out her muddled feelings. Darting over to the dressing table, she grabbed her handbag and knocked over the peace-offering, the cup of tea.

'Delia, where are you going?' Edmund demanded.

'I don't know,' she sobbed wildly. 'I don't want to see you. You've spoilt everything!'

She ran from the room and down the hallway. Maybe she hoped he would stop her from leaving as he had once before, but he didn't follow her and he wasn't leaning against the front door of the flat to prevent her from going through it.

She took the lift down to the ground floor and out in the lamplit softness of the summer night began to wonder why she was there. She almost turned back through the swing doors of the apartment building. Then she saw a red double-decker bus coming along the road. She ran to the nearby stop sign and signalled. The bus stopped and Delia climbed aboard.

She rode on the bus all the way to the terminus which was in a suburb and stayed on it, much to the conductor's surprise and concern, until it began its journey back into town. By the time it reached the street where she lived she had calmed down and was ready to apologise to Edmund for her silly, frantic behaviour.

She went up to the flat and opened the door and knew as soon as she stepped inside that he wasn't there. She sat up most of the night in the living room waiting for him to come. Next morning, her eyes burning through lack of sleep, she went to work, but every time the phone rang in the office she hoped it would be Edmund calling her to arrange to meet her for lunch.

He didn't phone and he didn't appear to ask Ben Davies if she could be allowed time off. Delia phoned the flat several times and found the ringing tone a depressing sound of defeat.

On the way home she bought his favourite foods and two bottles of wine. As soon as she entered the flat she called out his name. There was no answer and when she went into the bedroom there was no sign of him having been there.

In desperation she phoned Peter.

'Have . . . have you seen Edmund?' she asked.

'Yes, I have. As a matter of fact he's just left.'

'Oh.' Relief seeped through her. 'Then he'll be here in a few minutes.'

She heard him take a deep breath and clear his throat.

'No, I'm afraid he won't, Delia. He's gone away again. He left a message with me for you. Look, darling, why don't I come round to see you and talk to you? It isn't the sort of news I can pass on to you over the phone.'

CHAPTER TWO

THE sun was hot and yellow in a clear blue sky. Sparks of light, struck from the metal of the plane's wing, dazzled Delia's eyes and she looked away quickly, down to the expanse of Brazilian jungle far below, which spread like a cloak of rough green tweed over the land as far as she could see.

She still had no idea of what the jungle would be like. In her imagination it had always been a hazy, steamy jumble of dark dripping trees hundreds of feet high, completely impenetrable and inhabited by strange dark-skinned people, colourful exotic birds and slithery snakes.

Her arrival in Brazil had been quite official. She had been met at Rio de Janeiro's international airport by a group of people from the government department in charge of Indian affairs and had been installed in a luxurious bedroom in a huge hotel overlooking the famous Copacabana beach where she hadn't been able to sleep a wink all night because of the perpetual roar of traffic passing up and down the Avenida Atlantica.

Next day she had travelled with Professor Claudio Rodriguez, an anthropologist who worked as a liaison officer for the tribal protection service to Brasilia, and this morning at eight they had left the capital city of sparkling towers in this sleek silver plane. Now, several cups of sweet black coffee later, Delia was almost at her destination, Posto Orlando in the centre of the big jungle park which had been reserved for the primitive tribes of the Brazilian Indians.

She should be full of excitement and eagerness because she was about to visit places which many people would like to visit, but instead she was suffering from an attack of cold feet as she realised suddenly just how afraid she was of snakes, spiders and creepy-crawlies.

'We shall be landing in a few minutes. You had better fasten your seat belt,' said Professor Rodriguez, leaning across to speak to her. He was a swarthy middle-aged man with round dark myopic eyes behind thick-lensed glasses. Although shy, he had been kind and Delia tried not to show her distaste for the smell of garlic on his breath when he spoke to her.

The seven-seater Air Force plane made a bumpy landing on a rough air-strip which sliced through virgin forest. As she stepped down from the plane Delia had a glimpse of beehive-shaped huts with roofs made from palm fronds. A group of semi-naked Indians, all men, had come to greet the plane and standing with them was a squat grey-haired, grey-bearded man dressed in creased cotton shorts and shirt, a tall handsome younger man also dressed in shorts and shirt and, surprisingly, a shapely Brazilian woman with long black hair tied back simply at the nape of her neck and the most gorgeous golden tan Delia had ever seen.

The grey-haired man came forward, took Delia's hand in one of his and then to her great surprise pulled her into his arms and gave her the Brazilian *abraço*, an embrace which involved kissing her on both cheeks.

'Welcome, welcome at last,' he said in English. 'It is good to see the daughter of my old friend Frank Fenwick. I am Luiz Santos. May I present my nephew Manoel Santos, who is a sociologist working here with the tribes, and his wife Rita.'

Shaking hands with the handsome shy Manoel and his

wife, Delia glanced about her cautiously to see if Edmund was among the group of people. There was no sign of him.

'You are looking for Edmund?' queried Luiz, his dark eyes twinkling. 'I expect he is at the infirmary attending to the patients there. I can assure you I have kept our little secret and didn't tell him that the journalist who was coming to interview us was you. I haven't even told Rita and Manoel,' he added with a chuckle of mischief.

He told them now, quickly in Portuguese. They both looked amazed and then very amused, and Rita suddenly lost her shyness to exclaim in American-accented English:

'But Edmund is going to be so surprised too. We have been discussing what you would be like and he has made us laugh with his idea of a hard-boiled quick-talking woman journalist. We never expected anyone as pretty and feminine-looking as you. And of course we had no idea he had a wife.'

'How is he?' asked Delia, not hesitating to betray her concern for Edmund to these pleasant, interested people.

'I shall tell you as we walk along to the village,' said Luiz, who had been talking to Professor Rodriguez and issuing instructions to the Indians to help with the unloading of supplies from the plane. 'Come, it is not good for you to be standing out in this heat when you are not yet accustomed to it.'

Taking her arm, he guided her along a path between tall stems of thick grasses with edges as sharp as flick knives to follow a battered jeep which had been loaded with her baggage and boxes of medical supplies and which had brown-skinned Indian children clinging to it like monkeys.

'Edmund is much better than when I first wrote to you, I am glad to say,' murmured Luiz. 'But he is still too thin and he tires easily. He needs a rest, but he's determined to finish the work he came here to do and he won't go even to Brasilia or Rio for a change until it's done. I've tried to persuade him without success. Perhaps you will succeed where I have failed. Sometimes a wife, especially one as pretty as you are, can influence a man when all else fails.'

Delia gave him a startled sidelong glance. How little he knew about her relationship with Edmund!

'If he didn't tell anyone he had a wife how did you find out about me?' she asked.

'That was easy. When he turned up here at the post after walking from the site of the crashed plane he was so ill, raging with fever, I thought it was necessary to inform someone other than the organisation which sent him. I looked among his possessions and found his passport. As you know, at the back of it is a list of people, relatives or friends who can be contacted in case of emergency. Your name was at the top of the list with the address. I decided it was an emergency and wrote to you,' he explained.

His letter to her had come as both a surprise and a shock. It was the first news she had had of Edmund since he had dropped out of her life over sixteen months ago. Her first reaction had been to book a seat on the next plane flying to Brazil because the longing to see Edmund and to take care of him while he was ill had been overpowering.

Then she had remembered the circumstances of their last meeting and the fact that although they were married they were to all intents and purposes separated, and she had hesitated.

Anxious about him yet not knowing what course of action to take, she had worried. Worry had caused sleeplessness and once again she had fallen into that terribly depressed apathetic condition which had overcome her when she had realised Edmund had left her and had apparently disappeared off the face of the earth. She had become careless and absent-minded at her work, and Ben Davies had noticed.

One day when he was taking her to task for the mistakes she had missed when editing an article submitted to the magazine she had broken down in his office and all her worries about Edmund had come tumbling out.

His feet on his desk, puffing at his pipe, his grey eyes shrewd behind the smoke-screen, Ben had listened to her with surprising patience. When at last she finished he studied her silently for a while obviously considering the situation.

'You want to go and see him, don't you, girl?' he said in his slow Welsh drawl.

'Yes, I do,' she had confessed. 'But I don't see how I can go all that way. And I'm afraid that if he knows I'm coming he'll move on, disappear again . . .'

'But he's not going to know you're going to Posto Orlando,' he had interrupted her curtly, and she had stared at him in surprise.

'But how . . .?' she had begun, and had stopped when he smiled at her.

'You're going to see Luiz Santos, not Edmund,' he had continued. 'I'm promoting you here and now to the position of a contributing editor to the magazine. It's your first chance to follow in your dad's footsteps as a writer of geographical articles. By now you should know what we want and how to go about getting it. Of course you'll have to take Luiz Santos into your confidence a little and tell him that on no account is he to tell Edmund you're coming. I'll write to him also to tell him you're going to do a series of articles on that reserve for the tribes which he runs for the Brazilian government and remind him of the last time our representative visited him. I think you'll find he'll be very obliging when he knows you're Frank Fenwick's daughter. He and your dad thought along the same lines.' Ben had paused and sucked for a moment on his pipe, then had cocked an eyebrow at her. 'Any idea what Edmund has been doing out there?'

'According to Mr Santos he's been doing a tour of observation for an international organisation which is concerned with raising money for the provision of medical and other supplies for primitive people. The plane in which he was travelling crashed in the jungle and he was missing for a few weeks. He found his way to the Post where Mr Santos has his headquarters and is very ill,' she had replied.

'Humph,' Ben had grunted. 'Malaria, I expect. Oh, don't look so anxious, girl. He'll get better and by the time you fly out he'll be up and about. Now let's think. Who could he be doing the survey for?' He snapped his fingers. 'Got it! For O.S.P.P.' He reached for his phone. 'I'll get in touch with them and find out. They might also be interested in any articles you can write about the tribes. Now how soon can you be ready to leave for Brazil?'

And so the arrangements had been made and now she was here, walking towards a clearing where there was a collection of wooden and concrete huts, her heart hammering with anticipation at the thought of meeting Edmund and the sweat trickling down the backs of her legs under the pale green cotton trousers she was wearing.

It seemed that the arrival of the Brazilian Air Force plane with supplies was a social occasion. In a room in one of the wooden sheds Luiz and Rita passed round small cups of the thick sweet coffee which Brazilians apparently drink all the time to the pilots, the steward of the plane and Professor Rodriguez. In the doorway curious Indians crowded. They were tall muscular men with mahogany-coloured skin. Some of them had long black hair hanging down to their shoulders and wore woven brightly-coloured headbands to keep it in place. Others had their hair cut very short in circular fringes round their heads. Some wore tattered clothing. Others were almost naked and had painted their bare torsos and their broad-nosed, high-cheekboned faces with a thick orange-red paint.

When the brief spontaneous party was over, Luiz escorted the pilots, steward and Professor Rodriguez back to the plane and Rita took Delia to show her where she would sleep.

'Do you speak any Portuguese?' Rita asked, as they left the room and walked out into the yellow-bright humidity of the clearing and across the hard-baked reddish earth in the direction of another wooden shed built within the shade of some tall eucalyptus trees and banana palms.

'I tried to learn some before I came, but didn't have much time to pick up more than a few simple phrases,' replied Delia. 'And so far I haven't been able to understand what anyone has said to me in the language, so it's just as well some of you speak English or I'd be in terrible trouble. Where did you learn English?'

'At home. My mother is from the United States and spoke to us all in English from the time we were little children,' replied Rita. 'But you'll learn more of our language now you are here just by sitting with us and listening when we talk. I'll translate as much as I can to you. Edmund can speak Portuguese quite fluently now. Here we are.'

They went up a short flight of wooden steps on to a long verandah which had several doors opening on to it. Rita walked to the end of the verandah and opened the last door.

'This is Edmund's room,' she said. 'You and I were going to share the room next to it and Manoel was going to move in here with Edmund, but since you're Edmund's wife that won't be necessary now,' said Rita, smiling, her eyes glinting with amusement. 'I'm sure you're not going to object to sharing a room with your husband.'

'No, no, of course not,' said Delia quickly, but she wondered what Edmund would say.

The room was dark and stuffy because the window was screened by heavy wooden shutters. It was spotlessly clean and was furnished with two truckle beds festooned with white mosquito netting. A doorway in the corner led to a small lavatory which had a rusty shower and a wash basin with taps.

Delia's two travelling bags had already been placed in the room. She noticed the room was strangely bare of articles. Thre was only a travelling bag similar to her own on the floor at the end of one of the beds and it was fastened with a small padlock.

'We never leave anything lying about or our baggage unlocked,' explained Rita. 'It isn't that the people here are thieves in our sense of the word. They are so used to sharing everything with one another that they just assume that what is ours is theirs too. And don't expect too much privacy either. Look.'

Turning, Delia was surprised to see they had been followed into the room by several Indian men who were all staring at her and her baggage. Some of them stepped forward to touch her and she had to control an immediate desire to step away from them as they fingered the material of her blouse, touched her hair and admired the gold medallion she was wearing on a golden chain round her neck.

'They expect you to give them presents,' said Rita. 'Do you have any?'

Delia opened one of her bags and at once all the men crowded round her expectantly. She took out a bag of wrapped toffees and gave one to each of them. Grinning happily, they left the room, shedding toffee papers on the floor.

'I expect you'd like to wash, comb your hair and change your blouse before seeing Edmund,' said Rita considerately. 'I'll be in the next room. Tap on the door when you're ready.'

The wash in tepid water made Delia feel much better and she changed the blouse she had been wearing for a cotton halter top, wishing she had a lovely copper tan like Rita's. The paleness of her skin made her feel curiously naked as she walked beside the graceful long-limbed Brazilian woman back across the clearing to a large barn-like building with a roof but no walls. Hammocks swung from tree-trunks which supported the steeply pitched roof of palm fronds. Luiz and Manoel were both lying in the hammocks smoking cigarettes and talking.

'I hope you have your notebook with you,' said Luiz cheerfully to Delia as he slid out of his hammock. 'I'm going to show you round the Post now. You realise, I hope, that this isn't the only centre in the reserve, which covers an area of several thousand kilometres of the interior. But this post, called after my father, Orlando Santos, who conceived the idea of having a reserve where the tribes could be brought and would be able to live in their customary way without too much interference from white settlers, is the most important and it is here that we have the hospital. People who are ill in any of the outlying villages can be flown into here and looked after in the small infirmary. Small operations can be performed there. In fact we are very proud of it.'

The hospital was in a concrete building and the thickness of its walls prevented it from becoming too hot inside. In the large room which was its entrance hall and storage place a young Brazilian nurse looked up from the supplies she was unpacking. Luiz introduced her to Delia and asked her several questions in Portuguese. She answered and gestured to one of the doors on the other side of the hall.

'This way,' said Luiz. 'As I had thought, Edmund is here. We have been very glad of his presence because the doctor we had here had to go home on leave. Most of the doctors are usually volunteers from the medical schools in São Paulo and Rio and some of course from other countries like your husband.'

The nerves of Delia's stomach crawled as they walked across to the doorway and she had to force herself to appear cool and nonchalant in spite of the sweat which had broken out on her brow and the palms of her hands. The room they entered was long and was furnished by two rows of metal cots. Several of the cots were occupied by patients and by the one furthest away from the door a man was bending over the patient obviously examining him while another older nurse stood by.

A shaft of sunlight slanting in through a high narrow window, picked out glints of gold in the man's brown curling hair which had grown so long that he had confined it with a coloured headband like the ones Delia had seen some of the Indians wearing. A thin white shirt and a pair of frayed shorts which were really cut off jeans showed off the nut-brown colour of his sun-tanned skin.

As she and Luiz approached the bed Luiz spoke quietly in Portuguese. The man looked up sharply, his eyes flashing blue against the tan of his face. His glance shifted from Luiz to Delia and widened in surprise. His lean face seemed to go pale, but he said nothing, only stared.

'By God!' exclaimed Luiz. 'You're a cool one, Edmund. Do you not recognise this young woman?'

Edmund was recovering his poise rapidly. His gaze steady

on hers, he smiled slightly a little ironically. Hands clenched at her sides as she controlled a surging desire to fling herself at him and put her arms around him, Delia made her trembling lips smile back.

'Hello, Delia,' he drawled in his pleasantly-pitched soft voice. 'I won't pretend this isn't a surprise.' He glanced at Luiz and frowned. 'I thought you were expecting a journalist on today's flight.'

'This is she,' said Luiz dramatically. 'Your wife. She has come to interview us and when she goes back to England she will write articles about us for her magazine.'

'Is that true?' queried Edmund, looking at Delia again with his eyes sharpening with interest, but, unable to trust her voice, she could only nod. 'Good for you,' he went on. 'Congratulations on getting the assignment.'

'Thank you,' she whispered, thinking that whatever other faults Edmund might have no one could ever accuse him of being ungenerous. He had always shown an interest in her work at the magazine and had encouraged her in her ambition to be a writer like her father had been. 'How are you, Edmund?' she asked, aware of Luiz watching them. As Luiz had said, Edmund was too thin, but his eyes were clear and his skin looked healthy.

'Well enough,' he replied indifferently, and turned his attention to Luiz again. 'Why didn't you tell me Delia was coming here?' he demanded.

'I ... I ... asked him not to,' Delia put in quickly. 'I'll explain why later.'

'Yes, yes, all the talking between you can be done later,' said Luiz easily. 'We'll leave you now to finish what you were doing, Edmund. I'm just showing Delia round the Post. It is important that she sees everything in the short time she is here.'

As she left the room Delia longed to look back to see if Edmund was watching her, but she didn't because she decided that if she did she would betray to him that she wasn't as cool and collected as she was trying to appear.

Outside the infirmary the heat hit like a blow again and she hurriedly put on her sunglasses.

'I cannot understand,' Luiz exclaimed, shaking his grey head from side to side. 'You and Edmund, you meet and you do not embrace. Anyone would think you are not pleased to see each other. Are you not pleased to see Edmund?'

'Oh, yes, very pleased,' gasped Delia, who was having to cope with all sorts of confusing emotions but was glad she was able to say something without lying. She had been pleased to see Edmund again. She had been more than pleased, she had been overjoyed, and it was having to keep that joy under control which was giving her trouble now. 'But you see ... we ... we're not accustomed to showing how we feel in front of strangers,' she muttered, realising she had to make some attempt to explain.

'Aha. Now all is as clear to me as light,' said Luiz, much to her relief. 'I had forgotten that the English are shy about showing their affection for each other in public. The real reunion will come later, when you are alone together in your room. And that is how it should be, perhaps. Come now, I shall show you the hut of Kuru tribe which at present is living here at the Post. You must realise that each tribe is different in its habits and customs. Really they are not tribes so much as small nations, each one possessing different characteristics, in the same way as Europeans are different from each other. You understand?'

He led her into one of the beehive-shaped huts, indicating to her that she should lower her head to enter the narrow curved opening. After the brilliance of the sunlight outside it was very dark and even when she had removed her sunglasses she had difficulty in accustoming her eyes to the dimness.

But it was cool inside and the air smelt fresh and sweet. After a while she was able to make out two woven hammocks swinging from the sides of the walls. Only two Indians were in the hut, a man and a woman who were sitting on the floor cooking fish in a black pot over the embers of a fire, the smoke of which escaped through a hole in the dome-shaped roof.

When they left the hut they walked slowly back to the open barn, Luiz talking all the time, pointing and explaining. For Delia the heat and humidity were like a thick blanket coming between her and everything, blurring outlines and details and she was finding it difficult to concentrate on what he was saying. Every step made her break out in sweat and her throat felt very parched, so that when Luiz suggested that she rested in one of the hammocks in the shelter while he went to talk to the chieftain of one of the outlying villages who had come into the Post to see him she was very glad.

There was no one else in the barn to show her how to get into one of the hammocks. Going up to one of them, she noticed that it was closely woven from strips of tough-looking cloth not unlike hessian and was almost wide enough for two people to lie side by side. She sat down nervously on the side of it, hoping it wouldn't collapse and deposit her on to the floor when she eased herself into it.

'Take your shoes off when you lie in a hammock.' Edmund's voice was terse and commanding and she glanced up in surprise. He walked past her to the next hammock, kicked off the canvas shoes he was wearing and swung himself into the woven bed. Bending down, she unlaced the canvas baseball boots she was wearing and which she had bought in Brasilia at the suggestion of Professor Rodriguez as the best footwear for the jungle, and pulled them off, wondering how she was going to get them on again because, during her walk round the village, her feet had swollen with the heat.

Once she was in the hammock she found lying there very pleasant. A breeze wafted through from the river which she could see beyond the curve of a green bank. The water widened into a pool which was edged by sandy beaches and looked very inviting. On the other side of the pool there was no jungle but a stretch of bright yellow-green savannah dotted with small trees, like a park. Huge white and yellow butterflies the size of small birds kept swooping across the surface of the river and nearer at hand three green and yellow parakeets chattered and squabbled as they perched on the ropes which supported the hammocks.

But there was no peace after all. Mosquitoes zoomed about her head and began to nibble at her skin so that she had to slap at them.

Plonk! A packet of cigarettes landed on her knees followed by a box of matches. She looked round at Edmund. One bare leg and foot dangling over the side of his hammock, he looked thoroughly relaxed as he swung idly to and fro. Through the pale grey haze of cigarette smoke which drifted about him his blue eyes glinted at her with familiar derision.

'Smoking is the only way to keep the flies off unless you fancy covering yourself with the red paint the Indians use,' he said. 'Didn't anyone tell you to bring a supply of cigarettes with you?'

'Yes, but they're in my luggage,' she replied as she selected a cigarette from his packet and lit it awkwardly. She had never smoked and now the smoke caught in her throat, making her cough and causing her eyes to water. As she spluttered and choked she could hear him laughing.

How unkind he was, she thought miserably. It was strange that a man like him who had such compassion for the maimed and the sick, who felt so deeply about the less fortunate people of the world, could be unkind to her when he was supposed to love her. But perhaps he didn't love her and never had done, at least not in the way she had always wanted to be loved by him.

'Did you know I was here?' he asked her when she had finished coughing and had wiped her eyes.

'I didn't know where you were until I received a letter informing me as your next of kin that you'd turned up here after being missing in the jungle,' she parried warily, keeping in mind that he didn't know Luiz had written to her. 'Oh, Edmund, why didn't you keep in touch? Why didn't you tell me you were coming to Brazil?'

He gave her a puzzled glance and was silent for a few moments, still swinging idly in the hammock and blowing out smoke.

'Quite honestly I didn't think you were interested or would give a damn where I'd gone,' he replied coolly, at last. 'The last time I saw you I seemed to remember you were sorry I'd come back to you and that I'd spoiled everything for you by being there. Then you slammed out of the flat. When you didn't return I assumed you had meant what you said, so I left.'

She hadn't meant it. She had gone back later, contrite and humble and ready to make up, but he hadn't been there. At first she hadn't been able to believe Peter when he had come to tell her that Edmund had left her after only thirteen months of marriage. It was something which happened to other women, not to her. Then the reality of the situation had hit her, destroying her happiness and her self-confidence in one harsh blow as she realised she had created the situation by her own behaviour.

'I'm surprised to hear we're still married,' Edmund continued coolly, interrupting the flow of her thoughts. 'I'd have thought you'd have divorced me by now and would be married to Peter.'

'But I couldn't divorce you,' she replied in a small strained voice. 'I didn't know where you were.'

'That didn't have to stop you,' he retorted. 'I'm sure a slick lawyer like Pete could have arranged it all for you very conveniently.'

'He said he could, but . . . but . . . I asked him not to,' she muttered.

'Why?' How hard and cold he sounded, she thought miserably.

'B . . . because I wasn't sure . . . I couldn't be sure . . . I didn't know.' Her voice faded away to silence. In the face of his hostility she lost the courage to explain.

The sound of laughter drew her attention. A family of Indians were running past on their way to the river pool. The man, long-limbed and muscular, led the way and the woman followed him with five prancing, darting brown-skinned children. Watching them, Delia felt envy stir within her. How she wished such carefree happiness was hers!

Edmund's hammock rocked violently as he left it and shuffled his bare feet into his canvas shoes. *He's a bit of a hippy. Likes to go off and live in the jungle with primitive tribes.* Aunt Marsha's description of him echoed through her mind. In his frayed shorts and worn-out shirt with his curling hair confined by the Indian headband he fitted the description well. Possibly living here he had found what all hippies said they were searching for—peace, simplicity in the way of living and the minimum of possessions.

He came across to stand beside her hammock and looked down at her with critical assessing eyes.

'You look as if the heat is getting to you,' he commented. 'Would you like to go swimming?'

'Is it safe to swim in the river here?' she asked.

'It's fast flowing and clean. There might be a few stingrays hiding in the sand on the bottom, so don't stand still in the water, always keep your feet moving. I have my swimming briefs on under my shorts. If you'd like to go and change I'll meet you back here in about ten minutes. Do you know where your luggage is?'

'Yes, in your room. Rita arranged for me to sleep in there,' she said without looking at him. 'I hope you don't mind.'

'Why should I?' he countered carelessly. 'Now go and change, and don't forget to keep your shoes on coming down to the water. The grass and the ground everywhere is full of ticks and jiggers.'

Outside her room a group of Indians were sitting on the floor of the verandah. They stood up and followed her into the room when she unlocked the door, and for a moment Delia felt complete panic. Should she shout for help? Then she noticed they were pointing to her bags and remembered the sweets. Taking the packet out, she gave them one each and they left immediately, grinning and nodding their heads.

She closed the door and locked it from the inside, but while she was changing into her bikini she saw that they were peering at her through a crack in the shutters and they were still there waiting for her when she stepped outside and they followed her back to the barn where Edmund was waiting for her.

'I see you have a group of admirers,' he mocked as they

walked down to the strip of sand edging the river pool.

'It's the toffees I've brought that they admire, not me,' she replied. 'Talbot's Toffees,' she added with a grin, watching him pull off his shirt and drop his shorts to the ground. His time in the jungle and the subsequent illness had fined him down. There wasn't any fat on him at all and the bones of his rib-cage gleamed white through the tanned skin.

'Which sort?' he asked casually.

'The round ones with the white creamy centres. Can you tell me why the Indians like sweets so much?'

'It's because very little of what they eat is sweet. They don't use sugar and not many of them have fresh fruits. Don't give all those toffees to them, I wouldn't mind having some myself.'

He ran off into the water and Delia followed him, feeling a lift of spirits because she was with him and they were doing something which they both enjoyed—swimming.

The water was cool, and fresh. Parakeets flew above her head and butterflies landed on her wet shoulders. A hidden bird whistled among the trees and there was no sign of the stingrays about which she had been warned.

Floating on her back, Delia was startled by shouting. A group of mahogany-coloured Indian boys ran into the water suddenly and surrounded her, jumping, splashing and somer-saulting around her. They swam like brown fish and had a rubber ball which they batted to one another with their hands. One of them batted the ball to her. She tossed it back and at once she was part of their game and so was Edmund. Dog-paddling and diving, splashing and laughing, they played at water polo in the green and blue dappled water as if they hadn't a care in the world.

At last, breathless but happy, Delia walked out of the water to flop down on her towel on the sand. She felt refreshed, and although the noonday heat was very oppressive she didn't feel as thick-headed as she had when lying in the hammock.

She watched Edmund walk up the slanting sand towards her, the symmetry of his long legs set off by the white bikini briefs he was wearing. He sat down on the towel beside her stretching his legs before him and supporting himself on his arms which he stretched behind him.

'It isn't as good as swimming in the sea, but it's better than not swimming at all,' he commented. 'I thought often about the sea when I was lost in the jungle, half mad with insect bites and foul with sweat. I used to think about swimming in it and being cleansed by its saltiness.'

'Was it bad, being lost?' she asked.

'The worst part was the crashing of the plane and the realisation afterwards that I was the only survivor,' he replied in a low voice. 'Once I'd come to terms with that there was only one thought in my mind, and that was to find my way to this place as soon as I could. Fortunately the compass in the plane wasn't damaged and I had a good idea of which direction I should go.'

'How long did it take you to walk here?'

'Luiz tells me that it was about three weeks.' He shrugged. 'I had no idea of time and I was lucky. It's taken some people about two years to walk out of the interior.'

'Who was with you in the plane?'

'The pilot and two other people sent out with me by O.S.P.P. to assess the current situation of all the Indians living in this country, the ones in the cities as well as those still living in primitive communities or in this reserve. We were coming back here from Fenenal to finish the last part of the survey. What made it worse was that none of us had wanted to leave Fenenal. We'd had a fantastic time there living with two tribes.' He paused and flopped back on the towel, lifting an arm to shield his eyes from the sun. 'With Ingrid and Neil both dead I'm the only one left of the team to finish the survey.'

Delia glanced sideways at him, her ears tuned to every change in his voice. He sounded despondent.

'Were Ingrid and Neil also specialists in tropical diseases?' she asked cautiously.

'No. Neil was an anthropologist from the States and Ingrid was a sociologist, from Sweden, I believe. She was the most amazing person I've ever met.' Again he paused, then added so quietly that she only just heard, 'I still can't believe I'll never see her again.'

Delia quivered in reaction to that whispered cry from the heart. She wanted suddenly to know what the woman had been like. In her imagination she pictured a tall, blonde Amazon walking about fearlessly in the jungle and attracting Edmund's admiration.

She looked at him. He was very close to her, centimetres close, so that she had only to move her fingers slightly and she would touch his hard sinewy thigh. The need to touch him became an ache low down in her stomach. Now she could see his skin wasn't as clear as she had thought. It was marred by numerous insect bites. But where it was clear and softly furred with golden glinting hairs . . .

Shaken by the imperative desire to smooth her hand over the curve of his thigh in an intimate suggestive caress, Delia sprang to her feet. At once Edmund looked up at her from under the shade of his hand.

'What's the matter?' he demanded sharply.

'Nothing . . . I . . . I just thought I'd go back and put on some clothes. It's very hot sitting here,' she muttered. 'Can I have my towel, please?'

He came to his feet in one smooth movement, lifting the towel with him and handing it to her.

'I'll come with you. I need a clean shirt,' he said.

On the way to the hut where their room was they met Rita coming to tell them that lunch was ready.

'Why didn't you tell us you have such a pretty wife?' she said teasingly to Edmund, and looked a little puzzled when he didn't reply but walked past her as if he hadn't heard.

To Delia's relief there were no Indians lingering in front of the door to the room ready to follow her in and demand sweets or to peer at her while she changed her clothes. But Edmund was there, stripping off his briefs without any inhibitions before searching through his bag and finding a clean shirt and shorts.

Keeping her eyes averted from him, Delia opened her bag, laid it on the bed and took out another pair of cotton pants and another cotton blouse. Becoming aware that, as he zipped up his shorts, Edmund was watching her, she bundled the clean clothing under her arm and marched off to the lavatory, determined to change in there, guessing he would be laughing at what he had once called her 'unnatural modesty'.

There was a very small mirror above the wash basin and when she had dressed she peered into it. Her fine dark brown hair was a wet tangle and she had difficulty in dragging her comb through it. In the mirror a pair of black-lashed greyish green eyes set in a thin elfin face regarded her critically. They noted that her pink and white complexion was already acquiring a sunburn and that there was a sprinkling of tiny golden freckles across the bridge of her small neat nose.

She returned to the bedroom. Edmund was sitting on the edge of the bed which she had considered was hers. He was reading a newspaper which he had spread out. She recognised the paper as being one she had brought from Britain thinking he might be interested in reading it. The fact that he had it meant he had been in her luggage.

For a moment she felt angry and she wanted to tell him that he had no right to go into her bags without her permission. But the anger died down as she realised that to object would be a waste of breath. Like the Indians he believed in sharing everything. What was hers was his and what was his was hers, and the attitude had nothing to do with him being married to her.

He looked up and his glance, deeply blue, roved over her slowly.

'Rita is right. You are pretty. I'd forgotten how pretty,' he observed, and at once she was confused as she felt pleased because he still considered her to be pretty and irritated because he had forgotten and admitted frankly that he had. 'But Ben Davies must be out of his mind to send you out here to get a story,' he added.

She was tempted then to tell him that she was there because Luiz had invited her to come and see him, her husband, but there was still a hint of hostility in his attitude which made her hesitate.

'Why shouldn't Ben send me?' she countered. 'I've worked for him long enough to know what he wants in the way of an article. I've served my apprenticeship. He had to give me my chance some time.'

'I realise that,' and I'm sincerely glad he has given you a chance,' he replied. 'But he could have sent you somewhere else, somewhere which wouldn't have made such demands on you physically. This sweltering jungle isn't the place for you.'

'I can't see why it isn't,' she protested. 'Other women have come here and lived here. You've just told me about the sociologist who was with you in Fenenal. If she could travel about in the jungle and live with primitive tribes so can I.'

'Ingrid was exceptional,' he replied quietly, and looked down at the newspaper, seemingly more interested in it than he was in talking to her.

'Meaning that I'm not, I suppose,' she said in a choked voice, feeling jealousy of the dead woman awaken slowly and painfully within her.

'Not in the same way,' he said ambiguously, and the paper rustled as he turned a page.

'I don't believe it's anything to do with the jungle,' she accused wildly. 'You don't want me here because you don't want me.'

'What I want has nothing to do with it,' he replied roughly. 'You shouldn't be here.'

Disappointment because this reunion with him was so lacking in warmth and welcome and jealousy of a woman she didn't know and would never meet fused together in one overriding explosion of anger.

'Oh, you were always the same!' she flared. 'You never wanted me to enter this part of your life. Manoel Santos has his wife with him, but you've never wanted me with you. I had to stay behind in England. I was just a convenience, a woman you could sleep with when you came back because you didn't like sleeping alone, to stay with until you got "explorer's itch" again. You didn't really want a wife, and I've often wondered why you bothered to marry me . . .' Her voice broke and she had to jam her teeth into her lower lip to stop it from trembling. The tears she had vowed he would never see beaded her long eyelashes and her soft breasts rose and fell under the thin cotton shirt with the tumult of her feelings.

Edmund moved suddenly from the bed, coming to his feet with a lithe violence which was familiar and made her step backwards hurriedly, a purely instinctive defensive action. He noticed and his mouth twisted at one corner.

'It's all right, I'm not going to touch you. Some things I may have forgotten about you, but I haven't forgotten the way you reacted the last time I touched you,' he said between taut lips. 'I haven't forgotten either why I married you, but you seem to have done. Now if you're ready we'd better go and have some lunch.'

Stepping past her, he strode over to the door, yanked it open and walked out into the blinding yellow sunlight. Snatching up her handbag, Delia blinked away her tears and hurried after him, realising that she had no idea where the eating house was. With shaking hands she locked the door and ran down the verandah. By the time she caught up with him in the middle of the unshaded compound she was soaked with sweat again and her heart and head were both pounding after her hurried dash in the heat of the day.

They entered another long wooden hut near the barnlike building and where Luiz, Manoel, Rita and the two nurses were already sitting at a table with the chieftain who had come to visit Luiz.

Rita looked up, smiled in her friendly way and patted the empty place on the wooden bench beside her.

'Come and sit by me,' she suggested to Delia. 'You look flushed and hot. You haven't yet learned to take everything slowly.'

Delia sat down and a plate was passed to her and Rita told her to help herself to rice and beans from a big bowl.

'This is *manioc*,' she explained, spooning some glutinous-looking gruel for another large bowl on to the small heap of rice. 'It's made from a root which grows in the jungle. It's the staple diet of the tribes. Help yourself to one of the limes lying on the table and squeeze the juice into the water in your glass. You'll find it a very cooling drink as well as being necessary to your diet. We have very little fresh fruit.'

Everyone seemed to eat quickly as if very hungry and Delia found the food surprisingly tasty. Afterwards there were more glasses of coffee and of course cigarettes to keep the persistent mosquitoes away.

'And now a *siesta* in your room,' said Rita as they rose from the table and went outside into the humid heat again. 'When you've rested you're to come with Manoel, Edmund and me to a nearby village where an old man is ill. It will be interesting for you to see another tribe and how different they are from the one which lives here.'

Although she was glad of the chance to rest Delia found it was difficult to sleep, partly because the room was hot and airless and partly because of the confusion of her feelings.

Edmund hadn't come to lie on the other bed and she couldn't help thinking it was because he didn't want to be with her. Thinking of how they had snarled at one another before lunch it wasn't surprising, she thought miserably.

Oh, why had she come? What had she expected? An instant and ecstatic reconciliation in the same way she had found instant and ecstatic love two and a half years ago when she had first met him?

Too much time and distance had come between them for that to happen. He wasn't the same. He was a cool, wary stranger to whom she was bound in wedlock. Was it possible he thought she was different too?

CHAPTER THREE

In spite of the heat and the confusion of her thoughts Delia did go to sleep. When she opened her eyes again her heart jumped a little in apprehension because for a moment she didn't recognise where she was.

Then she remembered. She was at Posto Orlando and she had found Edmund and for the next few days she would be near him, living in the same place, sharing a room with him, able to talk to him at last.

A creaking noise alerted her. Raising her head, she saw that the door was opening slowly and she remembered, too late, that she should have locked it. A shaft of brilliant yellow light cut through the dimness and a figure appeared in the doorway.

'Are you rested?' asked Rita in a whisper. 'It's time for us to go.'

'Will I be all right dressed like this?' asked Delia, swinging her legs off the bed and pulling on the canvas baseball boots.

'Of course. Anything which is comfortable will do,' said Rita with a laugh. 'This isn't Rio, or New York or London. The worst sin in the jungle is for your clothes to look all new, not old. Don't forget to bring your notebook and your camera. Oh, and bring some presents for the tribe we're going to visit. Sweets and cigarettes are always popular. So is soap.'

'How long have you been at the Post?' Delia asked as they walked across the bright hot clearing to the battered jeep

58

which was parked in the shade of one of the huts.

'Almost six months. Always Manoel wants to be here, in the jungle working with his uncle. It is the sort of work he loves most, but I am always torn with longing to be here with him and another longing to be with our children.'

'Children?' exclaimed Delia. 'How many do you have?'

'Three, all boys, eight, six and four,' replied Rita, with a sigh.

'But who is looking after them while you're here?'

'My family, my mother and my sisters. They're well cared for—but oh, how I miss them!'

'Couldn't they join you here for the holidays?' asked Delia, thinking how much three boys could enjoy themselves here with the Indian children, swimming and hunting and playing.

'Manoel would like that, but I cannot take the risk. Everyone here has had bad malaria. Luiz has it every month and see how ill he is beginning to look. Manoel has had it more than once. And I have had it. For a young child to catch it would be fatal.'

'But the disease can be prevented now,' said Delia. 'I've brought pills with me to take every day which are supposed to prevent me from getting it.'

'As long as you have them and remember to take them you won't get it,' Rita assured her. 'But such drugs cost money. That's why your husband is here—to find out what funds are needed for supplying medicine. He'll make a report on the situation when he returns to England.' She shrugged her shoulders fatalistically. 'It won't be the first report made about conditions, but no one seems to act no matter how many reports.'

'I'm sure Edmund will try to get some action,' said Delia, surprising herself a little. She hadn't realised she had so much faith in Edmund's powers of persuasion.

Manoel was driving the jeep, so Rita sat beside him. Delia sat with Edmund on the back of the vehicle. Jekaro, a young handsome Indian who could speak Portuguese, went with them and held a shotgun across his knees. He was wearing an old-fashioned high-crowned, broad-brimmed straw hat pulled down over his long black hair. Edmund wore a similar hat and managed as always in spite of the raggedness of his shorts and shirt to look elegant. It was to do with the lean grace of his body and limbs and the fine chiselling of his facial features, Delia decided, feeling her love for him flare up suddenly within her, making her wish she could reach out and touch him.

'What's the gun for?' she asked him as the jeep rattled over the hard-baked ground of the clearing in the direction of the forest.

'One of the first laws of living in the jungle is that you must never go anywhere without a weapon because you might get lost and have to shoot an animal for food,' he replied.

'Did you have one with you when you were lost?'

'Yes. I took the one which was in the plane. Is that a hat you have in your hand? Put it on. It will protect your head from any insects which might fall from the trees.'

She pulled the hat on at once as they entered the jungle and followed a rutted track which twisted among giant trees festooned with creepers. It was cool and dim under the trees and there was a strong smell of damp earth. But it wasn't as frightening as Delia had imagined it to be and she was just thinking it was rather like taking a ride through an over-grown damp English wood when a large hairy insect fell on to her knee. At once she shrieked in revulsion and tried to brush it off with her hand.

'For God's sake don't touch it!' yelled Edmund. 'It's a centipede with poisonous hairs.' He produced a wicked-looking knife from a sheath at his belt, slid the point of the knife under the insect and flicked the hairy wriggling thing away. Behind her Delia could hear Rita and Manoel laughing and her cheeks burned with mortification.

'I always thought you'd be a liability in the jungle,' said Edmund to her in a low scornful voice. 'Why did you have to shriek like that?'

'I . . . I . . . couldn't help it,' she muttered. 'I can't bear the sight of creepy-crawlies and snakes.'

'I'm not over-fond of them myself,' he admitted, 'but I don't put on such a big performance when I come across one.'

'It wasn't a performance,' she protested. 'And it's not fair to say I'm a liability. I've only just come. This is my first time in the actual jungle and I haven't had a chance yet to prove that I won't be a liability.'

'You're not going to get any more chances, if I can help it,' he growled. 'You're going back tomorrow to Brasilia or wherever it was you came from this morning. When we get back I'll have a word with Luiz about it. All I have to say to him is that I don't think you have the physical stamina . . .'

'But that wouldn't be true,' she objected hotly. 'I'm as strong as you are. Anyway, as a doctor you should know that women are tougher than men and have more powers of endurance.'

'Some women have,' he corrected her coolly. 'But you're not necessarily one of them. You could get dysentery while you're here and in spite of all the precautions you could get malaria.'

'As if you cared,' she jeered at him shakily, once again close to tears because he seemed determined to reject her.

'Oh, I care all right,' he retorted. 'The medical staff at the Post have enough to do taking care of sick Indians without having you added to the number of patients in the infirmary.'

'Well, you can say what you like to Luiz, I'm not going back to Brasilia until I've done what I've come here to do, and that is to get enough information for those articles,' she retorted, glaring at him. 'You can't get rid of me as easily as that. Luiz is on my side.'

Edmund didn't say anything in reply, only gave her a strange ironic glance before looking away down the rutted path along which they had come. Shaking inwardly still as a result of the clash between them, Delia also looked away at the trees which were now pressing in around them, their branches seeming to strain upwards towards the light. Dead trees leaned drunkenly sideways, unable to fall downwards because ropes of creepers held them up. On the thick carpet of small plants which covered the ground red and blue flowers with thick sinister-looking petals made flashes of colour against the perpetual green.

They came to a clearing among the trees where the ground had been cultivated and maize grew in rows. In a stiff polite voice Edmund explained to Delia that it was called a *roca* and that the tribe made a new clearing every year for the growing of staple foods. A little further on he pointed out the previous year's abandoned *roca* already thickly overgrown by the ever-encroaching jungle.

Another twist in the path and they entered a clearing where three large oval huts with dome roofs were set round a small oblong hut. At the approach of the jeep thin dogs rushed out of the huts growling and barking and brown bare children ran for cover. As soon as the jeep's engine stopped the dogs stopped making a noise and the children crept back, staring at the vehicle and the people in it with round inquisitive eyes.

Tall muscular brown-skinned men wearing thick beaded belts and brightly feathered armbands, their faces thick with red paint, gathered round the jeep all talking at once in their strange high-pitched tonal language.

'They are very concerned about the old man and want Edmund and Manoel to go to his hut at once,' Rita explained to Delia. 'Jekaro is going to show us round the village.'

Delia remembered the presents she had brought. The sweets, cigarettes and small tablets of soap were accepted with cries of delight. An older woman came forward, took Delia by the hand and led her towards the entrance of one of the huts, gesturing to her to enter.

Inside the hut was cool and airy. Women sat about the floor. They were all working. Some were weaving baskets and others were stirring pots over low fires at each end of the room. Two young women with babies in their arms lay in swinging hammocks. Their bare skin was as smooth as satin and the colour of honey and their faces were almost hidden by curtains of long black hair.

'About twenty people live in each hut,' explained Rita to Delia, translating from what Jekaro was saying to her. 'Each family has its own area and stores its food and hunting equipment on those platforms in the middle of each area.'

'How quiet the children are,' remarked Delia. 'Not one of them is crying.'

'It's a sound I've never heard all the time I have been in the jungle,' said Rita. 'I believe it's because of the simple life their parents lead. They have few possessions and don't seem to want to want any more than they have already. This lack of pressure to acquire material goods gives them plenty of time to attend to their children, to be with them and to love them. Luiz says we can learn so much about living from them, and I think he's right. But oh, how I miss my own children and wish I could be with them. What shall I do, Delia? Leave Manoel and go back to them in Rio? Or bring them here and risk them catching a jungle disease? It's a terrible dilemma I'm in, yet not a new one.'

They left the hut, stepping carefully among the colourful macaws and parakeets which were scratching the floor for bits of food which had been dropped, out into the bright sunlight. The old woman who had led them to the hut pressed a parting gift into Delia's hand. It was a small beautifully woven basket, and seemed so much better than sweets or soap that Delia was overwhelmed by such generosity.

Edmund and Manoel were leaning against the jeep talking to a well-built, heavily painted young man who had feathers stuck in his hair. All three seemed to be very serious.

'He is the chief,' said Rita, once more translating Jekaro's explanation. 'You know, Delia,' she added in a more confidential way, 'I think that you are also in the same dilemma that I am in.'

'Oh! What do you mean?' exclaimed Delia. 'I haven't any children.'

'I know that, but you have a husband who likes living with and working for these primitive people as much as Manoel does. The government protection service has difficulty in finding doctors to work at the hospitals in the interior or who are willing to fly to out-of-the-way villages. It hasn't the funds to pay them, so most of those who come are young, inexperienced volunteers. There are very few who are as highly qualified as Edmund. I know that Professor Rodriguez has asked him to consider staying at Posto Orlando. If he decides to stay you'll have to decide whether you want to stay with him or go back to England, won't you?'

'I suppose I will,' muttered Delia, knowing that Rita was glancing at her with bright enquiring eyes as they walked across the clearing to the jeep. But deep down there was doubt in her mind. Already Edmund had shown he didn't want her at the post, not even for a short visit, so it seemed unlikely he would ask her to stay with him should he decide to offer his services to the Brazilian government department which looked after the tribes.

He didn't want her there. She could even see rejection of her in the way he took the seat next to Manoel in the jeep so that he didn't have to sit with her. She had come all this way in the hope of re-kindling the fire of love which had once blazed between them, but it seemed very much as if there was nothing left, only cold ashes.

She felt depressed and subdued as they drove back through the fast-dimming green light, passing a group of Indian hunters returning to the village from the depths of the forest, bows and rifles slung over their shoulders and arrows clutched in their hands, strangely romantic figures who disappeared almost as suddenly as they had appeared, melting into the darkness of the forest.

At the Post supper was ready and she was hungry enough to find beans and rice with some fried fish tasted delicious. While they were eating Luiz put forward his plans for her during the next few days and she sat listening to him, watching Edmund's lean enigmatic face, waiting for him to do what he had threatened to do, suggest to Luiz that she should return to Brasilia the next day.

'We shall go to Binauros by river,' said Luiz. 'Then you will see how beautiful the jungle can be. It will take us two days to get to the other post and on the way we'll spend one night sleeping out. You will stay there another two days and then fly back here to catch the next supply plane returning to Brasilia. While we are at Binauros there will be an opportunity for both of you to fly to one of the most inaccessible villages in the park where you will stay with one of the most attractive of the tribes.' He turned with a smile to Edmund. 'And when that is all over, my friend, it will be time for you to return to civilisation and put in that report of yours from which we are hoping so much.'

Edmund flicked out the match with which he had just lit a cigarette, inhaled and blew out a cloud of smoke to deter the persistent mosquitoes before he spoke.

'I have to admit I don't want to leave and go back to civilisation,' he said. 'Being here, living here and in Fenenal and all the other places has been a tremendous experience for me. For the first time in my life I've come near to living as I always wanted to live, simply and naturally.' He drew hard on his cigarette and the smoke curled in grey spirals about his face. 'There were times, particularly in Fenenal, when it seemed like paradise on earth,' he added.

'Ah, no,' said Luiz, laughing. 'We have saved paradise for you until now, to visit in the company of your pretty wife. This journey we shall take down river to Binauros and the flight to the other village will be a second honeymoon for you both. May I suggest, Delia, that you go to bed now? It has been an exciting day for you and you're tired. We shall be leaving at dawn. Sleep well.'

Although reluctant to leave the table while Edmund was still there with Luiz in case he should attempt to persuade the kindly Brazilian to send her back to Brasilia the next day, Delia had to admit she felt tired, so she said goodnight and walked across the moonlit clearing to the sleeping hut.

The tiny room was still hot and two mosquitoes were

droning around the bare electric light bulb which lit it. She sprayed the room with insecticide to get rid of them. While she was preparing for bed the light went out suddenly and she assumed the generator which supplied the current had been switched off for the night.

The smell of the spray tickled her nose and the bites on her legs and arms itched as she lay in the darkness between damp sheets. A second honeymoon—Luiz' laughing remark had seared her. What chance was there of a second honeymoon for her and Edmund when there was such a wide gulf between them? The months they had spent apart were a much longer period of time than they had ever spent together.

Mentally she calculated the days and weeks she had lived with Edmund. Barely four months out of two and a half years of marriage. Was it any wonder she understood him so little? But then when they had been together had she bothered to try and understand him?

No, she had to admit that she hadn't. As long as he had been with her, as long as he had come back to her and had made love to her nothing else had mattered. The one time he hadn't treated her with gentleness and consideration, the one time he had shown that he could behave violently she had reacted in an immature way. She hadn't even tried to listen to his attempts to explain why he had behaved the way he had.

The door of the room opened and closed. The beam of a powerful torch flickered over her bed, then wavered about as Edmund moved into the room. She heard him swear as he stubbed his toe on her luggage which was lying on the floor. Then the beam of the torch lit up the entrance to the wash room as he went in there. Water gushed and tinkled as he washed. The beam of light slanted back into the room, came very close, then illuminated the ceiling when he placed the torch on the small table between the two beds. There was the plonking sound of shoes being dropped to the cement floor, the rustle of clothing being taken off. The other bed creaked when he lay down on it and the torch went out.

For a few moments there was a heavy silence. Then Edmund's bed creaked again.

'Delia,' he whispered. 'Are you awake?'

'Yes.'

'I'd like to know why you asked Luiz not to tell me you were coming here,' he said. 'You said you'd explain.'

She licked her lips which were suddenly dry. Her head was pounding with pain and her tongue felt thick as a result of the still oppressive heat. She wished she had the courage to tell him why she had come, but she was afraid of being rejected again.

'I . . . I . . . thought that if you knew I was coming you'd leave the Post,' she muttered.

'And would that have mattered?' he asked.

'Well . . . er . . . yes. It would have mattered very much to the people who are depending on you to make that report to O.S.P.P.,' she replied, quite truthfully, remembering the conversation she had had with the chairman of the organisation before she had left England. On no account, he had said, was Edmund to be upset or prevented from finishing the survey of the health of the tribes and the situation regarding medical supplies. The survey had been held up for various reasons, such as Edmund being lost in the jungle and the death of the other two members of the team, and the chairman hoped she would be able to persuade Edmund to return to England and make his report as soon as possible.

'Is that the only reason?' Edmund queried, and she thought she detected a note of despondency in his voice.

'Yes. O.S.P.P. would like that report soon,' she said warily.

'I know. They'll get it in due course,' he said.

'You are going back to England, then?' she asked.

'Not if I can avoid it.'

'Oh, but Edmund, you must!' she exclaimed.

'Why must I?'

'To make the report.'

'I can send it from here.'

'But that won't be the same,' she said urgently, sitting up in bed and trying to see him in the darkness, but it was impossible to penetrate the gloom. 'Surely you can see that. Much more notice will be taken of the report if you can present it in person. Mr Tyson said I was to tell you that.'

'Shush! Keep your voice down. The walls are thin. Manoel and Rita are next door to us and they'll be able to hear everything you say,' he whispered fiercely.

'I don't care if they do,' she countered, but lowered her voice just the same. 'Why don't you want to go back to England?'

'Because there's nothing there for me to go back to,' he replied, and she felt as if he had driven a knife into her heart. 'And there's something for me to do here. I'm needed here and can do the work I'm trained to do. And having a private income I don't have to be paid to do it.'

She was silent while she coped with the pain which was racking her. Tears welled in her eyes and she bit her lip hard. The rejection she had feared a few minutes ago had happened. *Nothing in England for him to go back to.* Apparently it had never crossed his mind to go back to her.

'By the way,' he drawled sleepily, 'I asked Luiz to send you back to Brasilia tomorrow, but he refused, God knows why. I hadn't the heart to tell him that neither of us is interested in having a second honeymoon, so the trip to Binauros is still on.' He laughed shortly. 'Come to think of it, we never had a first honeymoon, did we?' He yawned suddenly and the bed creaked again as he moved. 'G'night,' he muttered.

Delia didn't reply. She was afraid he would hear that she was crying. After a while she could tell by the regular sound of his breathing that he was asleep. But she couldn't sleep. She was too tormented by her thoughts as well as by the heat and the bites on her body which itched and itched. She tossed and turned, becoming hotter and itchier than ever.

At last she gave up and sitting up in bed groped for the torch. She found it and clicked it on. Moving as quietly as possible, she slipped off the bed and went over to the one chair where she had left her handbag. Tiptoeing back to bed she shone the torch for a few seconds on the other bed. Edmund was lying on top of the thin blanket and he was wearing only underwear briefs.

Directing the torch's beam back to the table she found a bottle of sterilised water, opened it and poured a little into a glass. She took a small phial of pills from her handbag and shook one pill into her hand. Tossing the pill into her mouth, she washed it down with a little of the water.

Taking a tip from Edmund in the hopes of feeling cooler, she stripped off her nightdress and pushed it under her pillow. She covered herself with a sheet only and lay down again, closing her eyes determinedly. Slowly the pounding of her heart and head eased as the pill took effect and she slipped into a deep sleep.

She was awakened suddenly by the feel of a hand on her shoulder shaking it and the sound of a voice calling her name. The hand left her shoulder and suddenly the sheet was twitched away from her. She opened her eyes in alarm

and snatched the sheet back to gather it round her naked-
ness. The shutters were open and the room was full of pale
grey light and Edmund was standing by the bed looking
down at her. He was wearing a long-sleeved sun-faded dark
blue shirt and long white cotton pants and he was standing
with his hands on his hips and his eyes were dancing with
devilment between thick bronze-coloured lashes.

'Why did you pull the sheet off me?' she demanded
crossly. Her head was heavy and she longed to lie down
again to continue sleeping.

'It was the only way I could get any reaction from you,' he
replied. 'You and I have a date this morning to go down
river and it's time you were moving about and packing your
bags.' He bent forward from the hips to stare more closely at
her, first at one of her eyes and then the other. 'You look
pretty groggy,' he remarked. 'And you were sleeping
heavily. You look drugged.' His voice sharpened on the last
word and he turned to glance at the table. The phial of pills
was lying there in full view. 'Did you take one of these last
night?' he demanded curtly, flashing an icy glance in her
direction.

'Yes. I had a headache and I couldn't sleep.'

'Do you often take one?'

'Only when I can't sleep.'

He didn't say anything but sat down suddenly beside her
on the edge of the bed and taking her left wrist curved his
fingers about it to feel her pulse while he stared at his wrist
watch.

The gentle touch of his fingers on the thin skin of her
wrist, the warm male smell of him in her nostrils, the sight
of golden brown skin against the blue of the half-buttoned
shirt went to her head. She swayed slightly towards him,
aware suddenly of her own bareness. Desperately she

clutched the folds of the rough sheet against her breasts as she fought against a desire to cast it aside and fling her arms about him and press herself against him.

The feeling made her shake. He felt the quiver and gave her a sidelong glance from beneath his lashes.

'What's the matter now?' he drawled.

'N ... nothing.' Her tongue seemed to want to stick to the roof of her mouth when his eyes glinted with scepticism. 'I'm perfectly all right,' she insisted, 'so don't you dare go and tell Luiz that I'm not, Doctor Talbot.'

'The way you're quaking anyone would think you'd never been examined by a doctor before,' he retorted with a sardonic twist to his mouth as he released her wrist. 'Your pulse is sluggish, but that's not surprising after taking one of those. You're not going to take any more,' he added, rising to his feet and scooping the phial up in his hand so he could study the label. 'A young woman like you shouldn't have to take anything like this to sleep. Who prescribed them for you?'

'A doctor in London.'

'Why? Have you been ill?' He sat down beside her again and was looking her over with such an expression of concern on his face that she found it difficult not to give into a longing to rest her head against his shoulder and tell him everything.

'In a way,' she muttered.

'What way?' he persisted.

'I'm not going to tell you. It ... It's none of your business,' she replied defensively.

'Yes, it is. Come on, tell me.'

'Why should I?' she countered, flinging her head back so she could glare at him. 'You never tell me anything about yourself. Why do you want to know? Because you're a doctor or because you're my husband?'

His eyes blinked twice as if he had been struck in the face and bone gleamed whitely through the taut freshly shaven skin of his jaw.

'When were you ill? Recently?' he asked quietly.

'I'm not going to tell you,' she replied stubbornly.

Now the room was filled with rose-tinted pearly light as the sun came up. Tension twanged between them as they stared at each other. Then Edmund stood up and turned away.

'All right, have it your own way,' he said. 'But you're not going to take any more of these pills.'

Before she could object he strode towards the wash room, the phial of pills in his hand. Gasping at his arrogance, Delia got out of bed, grabbed the clothes she had been wearing the day before and dressed quickly. She arrived in the wash room in time to see the last pill being washed down the outlet in the basin.

'You had no right to do that!' she accused furiously.

'Of course I had,' he retorted curtly. 'On two counts. As a doctor and as your husband.' Pushing past her, he strode back into the bedroom. 'I'll make sure you haven't any more of them tucked away.'

Turning, she followed him across the room in time to see him take hold of her handbag and tip it upside down so that all the contents fell out of it on to the table. Angrily she flung herself across the room to snatch at the bag and to collect up her scattered belongings.

'You . . . you . . . Oh, how dare you!' she choked, scarcely able to speak, she was so angry, but he had turned away and looking round she saw he had unzipped her travelling bags and was tossing clothes out of them.

'I haven't got any more sleeping pills, only pills for malaria,' she shouted at him, careless of whether Rita and Manoel could hear her. 'Please leave my things alone!'

Edmund ignored her, searching the bags thoroughly before tossing the articles of clothing back into them, not worried whether they were folded or not.

'Oh, look at the mess you've made of everything!' she wailed, going down on her knees by the bags and taking the clothes out again.

'You can pack when you've had breakfast,' he said crisply. 'And put your boots on. Never walk anywhere without them.'

'I . . . I'd no idea you could be so bossy and arrogant,' she seethed as she pulled on her boots.

'Well, you know now,' he returned coolly. 'There's a lot I don't know about you too, so the next few days are going to be interesting as we get to know each other, aren't they? Now come and get your morning coffee before the others drink it all.'

The longing for coffee fought a battle with a longing to defy his brusque orders and won. Scowling mutinously, Delia followed him across the compound. It must have rained heavily in the night, for the ground was covered with muddy puddles from which a faint white mist was rising as the sun, already hot, began to suck up the water. Parakeets and macaws were chattering noisily as they perched on the roofs of the huts, but there was no sign of any people.

There was no one in the eating room either.

'I thought Luiz said we were going to leave at dawn,' exclaimed Delia as she sipped hot sweet white coffee which Edmund brought her from the kitchen. 'According to my watch it's past eight now.'

'By dawn he meant four or five hours later,' said Edmund with a grin as he took a seat opposite to her. 'Another Brazilian would know he meant that. You'll get used to the casual attitude to time. Here there are no deadlines to be met, no trains or buses to catch.' He gave her an underbrowed searching glance. 'You know, living here even for a few days might do you some good, relieve that hyper-tension you seem to be suffering from.' He struck a match and put the flame to the cigarette he had inserted in his mouth. 'It'll do you far more good than those pills you've been taking.'

What would he say if she told him that the hyper-tension had been caused by worry about him and by over-indulgence in vain regrets about their estrangement?

'I thought you didn't want me to stay,' she retorted challengingly.

'That was yesterday. I feel differently today,' he replied tantalisingly. 'You're here, we're going on a journey together and there isn't anything I can do about changing the plan.' He shrugged his shoulders and smiled across at her, the first time he had smiled properly since she had arrived, and she felt her knees go weak. 'What will be, will be,' he added. 'Have you a long-sleeved shirt you can wear? There isn't much shelter from the sun on the river boat and even if long sleeves make you feel hot they're preferable to having scorched skin.'

Everything he said seemed contradictory. He didn't want her to be with him, yet he kept showing concern for her welfare as if he felt responsible for her, reluctantly responsible.

Delia looked at him from under her lashes. The last year spent mostly in the jungle had carved changes in his lean face. He looked older and wiser and sadder. Yes, that was it. There was a sadness in his face which hadn't been there before, the same sadness which was in Luiz' expression. What had put it there? The suffering he had seen among the simple primitive people of the tribes who had been uprooted from their land and wrenched from their way of life by the white settlers? Or was it the plane crash and the death of his team-mates? In particular the death of the woman Ingrid.

'Where is Fenenal?' she asked.

'West of here. It's an island in the middle of a huge river. It's very beautiful, completely untouched. Two tribes live there. Contact was made with them only a few years ago by a Brazilian explorer called Pedro Silveira,' he said.

'Why did you say it seemed like paradise on earth?'

'Because living there was so uncomplicated and we were cut off completely from the rest of the world. No regular supply flight, no radios. Time lost all meaning.' He sighed and his eyes, slitted against the smoke rising from his cigarette, looked past her as if he were seeing something which wasn't there.

'Did Ingrid feel like that about the place too?' she asked, feeling envy stir within her again.

'She might have done,' he replied, giving her a puzzled glance, 'although I never heard her say so.'

'What did she look like?' she asked impulsively, and his eyebrows went up in mocking surprise.

'What's this? An interview for *Geography Illustrated*?' he scoffed. 'Would details about Ingrid made your articles about the jungle more interesting for the women readers of the magazine, be a sop to the women's liberation groups?'

She couldn't control the surge of pink colour to her cheeks betraying that her interest in Ingrid was personal rather than objective. Edmund's eyes narrowed suspiciously, then were hidden as he looked down. He sighed and the slight sound so expressive of a feeling of regret stabbed through her.

'All right,' he said. 'I'll tell you about her. She was small, smaller than you are and very slight. Her hair was fairish and cut short. It fell forward in a wave over her forehead and she had a way of running her fingers through the wave, pushing it back when she was excited. She had grey eyes, large ones which seemed to shine with goodness, and she had very sound white teeth which she showed a lot when she laughed.' He paused, leant an elbow on the table and shaded his eyes with his hand. 'She was beautiful in every way,' he added in a low voice. 'Both Neil and I loved her.'

Shock tore through Delia. Hardly aware of what she was doing, she groped for his cigarette packet and took a cigarette. He held a lighted match to the end of the cigarette for her and she met his scornful glance.

'That's really what you wanted to know, isn't it?' he jeered. 'Just as you wanted to know once if I found Marsha attractive. Well, now you know I loved Ingrid, and so did everyone else who knew her. She was that sort of person. But it doesn't mean I slept with her or had a love affair with her. We were friends working together, living in a close-knit tribal community. And since you're so keen on lurid details, she was older than I am—about eleven or twelve years older. Now is there anything else you'd like to know? Or can you make up the rest using that over-active imagination of yours?'

His scorn had a crushing effect on her and the taste of tobacco smoke was bitter in her mouth, but no more bitter than the taste of humiliation.

'My imagination isn't any more active than yours is,' she retorted. 'You imagined once that I was having an affair with Peter.'

'And could still be having one for all I know,' he jibed nastily. 'But your memory is letting you down again. You've forgotten that I had a fact, a personally-observed fact on which to build my theory about the relationship between you and him. I saw the two of you making love . . .'

'We weren't making love,' she denied hotly.

'Weren't you? Then what the hell were you doing?' he queried harshly.

'I tried to tell you at the time, but you wouldn't listen,' she flung at him.

'And later, after you'd gone I heard it all from the great lover himself,' he said dryly.

'From Peter?' she exclaimed.

'Yes, from Peter. I went to his place that evening to see if you had gone there.' He selected another cigarette from the packet and lit it with the one he had finished smoking.

'What did he say?' she asked.

'Oh, he was very pleasant, surprised when I asked for you, but pleasant. Invited me in so we could talk it over in a civilised fashion as friends should, and he pointed out in that calm practical way of his how crazy it had been for an un-domesticated freewheeling type like me to get married in the first place.' He rubbed at his chin and slanted her a mocking glance. 'I couldn't help but agree with him. I knew at the time I married you that the balance of my mind was disturbed.'

'Was that all he said?'

'No. He told me you were unhappy,' he said flatly.

'And you believed him?' she exclaimed. 'Oh, Edmund, how could you?'

'It wasn't difficult after what had happened between us at the flat,' he replied dourly. 'You'd fought me off as if I were a stranger instead of your husband just home after putting in several weeks of celibacy in the most God-awful scenes of devastation I'd ever seen in my life.' He smiled rather wearily as she looked up sharply when he mentioned celibacy. 'Oh, yes, I was faithful to you while I was away, both times. A lot of good it did me,' he added.

'I was frightened. You were so angry. I'd never seen you angry before,' she whispered defensively, thinking all this should have been said fifteen months ago. If both of them had been more loving perhaps all the long months of soul-searching and unhappiness would have been avoided.

'At the time I thought I had every right to be angry,' he said slowly, reflectively. He laughed a little self-mockingly. 'You know, I behaved conventionally possibly for the first time in my life. I reacted to the age-old situation of the husband coming home to find his wife in the arms of her lover in an age-old way.'

'Peter wasn't my lover,' she asserted as loudly as she could without drawing the attention of the two Indians in the kitchen.

'According to him he was,' he drawled.

'He was lying, honestly he was, Edmund. I used to go out with him when he invited me because he assured me you wouldn't mind and that you had in fact suggested it to him. Did you?'

'Not in as many words. I might have said casually "watch out for Delia for me", but I didn't suggest he should act as a "shadow husband". That was entirely his idea,' he replied. 'I don't think I did mind that first time I was away. I trusted you and I trusted him until that evening, and then suddenly I found myself in a situation which I'd always resolved to avoid if possible.' He gave her a hard level look across the table. 'The sort of situation I'd seen my father caught in twice,' he added softly and bitterly.

'Oh! You mean your mother . . .?' Delia gasped, and her hand went to her mouth. 'I didn't know.'

'Of course you didn't know, because I never told you.'

'I wish I had known, though,' she said thoughtfully. 'If I'd known that I might have understood why you were so angry. But Peter should never have told you I was unhappy. Did he tell you why he thought I was?'

'He said you expected more from marriage than you were

getting from me. He said you needed the sort of husband he could be, who would come home every night at five, would buy you a house you could furnish together with a garden you could dig in together and would give you the children you could rear together.' He broke off with a crack of laughter and raked a hand through his hair as he shook his head. 'Hell, it was quite a lecture on my shortcomings! By the time it was over I was convinced I'd committed a sin against you by marrying you and should get out of your life as quickly as possible before I messed it up any more. So I did.'

'Peter had no right to tell you that,' she complained miserably. 'And you—oh, you had no right to believe him or to go off the way you did without telling me where you'd gone. Oh, why did you, Edmund? Why did you?'

'I deserted you, darling,' he said with a sardonic lift of his upper lip as he crushed out the remains of his cigarette in the tin lid which was used as an ash-tray. 'The idea was to make it easier for you to get a divorce. Didn't Pete tell you?' He swung off the bench and stood up. 'I want to look at the patients in the infirmary before we leave. You'd better go and pack your bag so you'll be ready when Luiz appears and says it's time to go.'

He went out, and Delia sat sipping the last of her coffee, thinking over all that he had said. So much had been explained. Now she knew why he had left her. Peter, his best friend, had convinced him that she didn't want him any more.

But he might not have been so easily convinced if she hadn't run out on him that evening or if she had returned. Delia groaned and for a moment clutched her head between her hands in an agony of remorse and regret as she recalled her own outraged behaviour. If only she had been more loving; if only she had responded to him instead of taking fright; if only, if only ... There, she was doing it again. Wasting time in regrets instead of taking action.

What action should she take? How could she show Edmund she was sorry so many months after the event? How could she approach him when he was so obviously not in love with her any more? How could she undo the damage Peter had done to the beginnings of a tender passionate relationship which might have grown into a strong trusting love?

Voices at the door of the room made her look up. Luiz and Manoel were coming in. They greeted her and after fetching coffee sat down at the table.

'The engine of the boat is old and a little temperamental,' Luiz said. 'Manoel has been persuading it to go. We would like to have a new faster boat for visiting the river-bank villages, but there isn't any money for one. You might mention it in one of your articles and maybe some kind person somewhere will read it and donate a boat to us. Are you ready to go?'

'Not quite. I have to pack my bags,' replied Delia, rising to her feet.

'Bring one only with you containing enough clothes for a few days. Lock everything else in your other bag, because you'll be returning here. I'll send Jekaro along to your room to carry the bag down to the boat for you.'

CHAPTER FOUR

THE boat in which they were going to travel down river was long and narrow. The engine was in the middle of it and was covered by a long flat roof supported by poles making the craft resemble an old-fashioned pleasure boat more suitable for a pleasant Sunday afternoon outing than for a voyage along an important waterway.

The luggage was stored with boxes of medical supplies under the roof where there were also two long benches for passengers to sit on. Since Luiz and Edmund seem to have taken over the benches and were engaged in what seemed to be a very earnest conversation about anthropology Delia and Rita climbed on to the top of the roof to sit under the burning sun, while Manoel, Jekaro and Mejai, who were both from Binauros, took turns at steering the boat and looking out for submerged sandbanks.

The river was wide and at first the water was a clear brown, but they hadn't gone far along it when it was joined by another river and the colour changed to a murky greyish-green.

'Why has it changed colour?' Delia asked Rita. Seated cross-legged wearing her floppy-brimmed white linen hat, she had her notebook at the ready and her camera near at hand.

'There are two kinds of river in the jungle,' Rita explained. Wearing only a very brief bikini which showed off her shapely golden-skinned figure, she did not seem in the least bothered by the heat of the sun. 'One we call "black" and the other "white". The white ones like the one we're following now contain more disease and insect life than the black. You're more likely to get malaria by being bitten by a mosquito on this river, so I hope you've taken your pills today.'

In the fuss with Edmund Delia had forgotten to take the malaria pills, so she searched her handbag for the phial containing them, but was unable to swallow them because there didn't seem to be anything to drink.

'Jekaro will be making coffee soon on the little spirit stove,' said Rita. 'You'll be able to take them then. Oh, isn't it lovely and peaceful gliding along in this way!'

It was. The engine made a reluctant put-put sound and the boat seemed to drift with the fast-flowing water rather than be pushed along. Thick trees, a thousand shades of green, fringed the banks of the river, rimming it with a reflection of green. Sometimes the banks became cliffs of red earth and the reflection changed to a dark crimson colour.

Where the river widened it was often split by smooth sandbanks gleaming golden in the sunlight over which swarms of tiger-striped butterflies fluttered in perpetual dance. Crocodiles lay on the banks basking in the sun, slipping into the water to hide when they heard the approach of the boat. Kingfishers were flashes of sapphire against the green of the trees and large white herons with curved necks and long thin legs flapped wide wings across the reflection of cloudless blue sky.

The sun blistered down and Delia was glad of her long-sleeved shirt and long pants even though she felt hot. She was glad too she had brought plenty of protective skin lotion to smear on her face and hands.

Time passed peacefully and effortlessly. With so much natural beauty to watch and nothing to do it was easy to relax. Once, feeling the need to escape from the sun's rays, Delia scrambled off the roof into the engine room, but found it was even hotter there and that the fumes from the engine were sick-making. Both Luiz and Edmund were stretched out on the benches and both seemed to be dozing. Going back to perch on the roof again, she stared at the bright water and wondered if it would be possible to swim.

At that moment, as if in answer to her thought, the engine of the boat coughed wheezily and stopped. Manoel went to attend to it, to take out plugs and clean them and to empty the carburettor. The boat drifted sideways on the swirling current and the sun seemed hotter than ever.

'Couldn't we swim?' said Delia hopefully to Edmund, who had come up from the engine room to sit on the roof.

'Not here,' said Luiz, who had also appeared. 'The water is thick with piranha.'

'They only bite if they smell blood,' argued Edmund. 'In Fenenal we often swam in piranha-infested rivers.'

'But you are not going to swim here, my friend, while you are under my supervision,' said Luiz. 'Nor is Delia.'

'Oh, it's all right,' said Delia quickly. Even though she was longing to be in the water the mention of the dreaded man-eating fish had put her off completely. 'Is there any other way I could cool off?'

'If you would like to put on your bikini we could scoop up water from the river and pour it over each other,' suggested Rita.

'What a good idea!' exclaimed Delia, and within seconds had her shirt and pants off to show she had had the fore-thought to wear her bikini under them.

Laughing and joking, they scooped up water in the tin cans Jekaro had found and poured it over each other and sat dangling their feet in the smoothly swirling water. It was a good alternative to swimming and feeling much cooler Delia was able to enjoy the simple meal of tinned sardines, sweet wholemeal biscuits and the inevitable sweet black coffee which Mejai was able to produce.

The engine spluttered into life again and the boat chugged on through the blinding brilliance of the afternoon. Delia smothered her skin with protective lotion and risked sunburn, hoping she might acquire a deep coppery tan like Rita's.

She had been lying out on the roof for only a short while when she felt a movement beside her and looking round and up saw that Edmund had come to sit beside her and dangle his legs over the edge.

'Put your shirt and trousers on,' he said, pitching his voice low so that none of the others could hear what he was saying. 'You're going to look like an over-ripe tomato if you don't,' he added, dropping her creased cotton clothing on her knee. 'You're also going to get sunstroke. Have you no sense? Do I have to tell you what to do all the time as if you were a child?'

Under the shadow of the brim of his old straw hat his blue eyes were hard and critical as their glance roved over her, and once again she felt the effect of his hostility. It was like being punched, she thought, her spirits which had been lifted somewhat by the pleasant relaxed journey plunging down to an all-time low.

'No, you don't,' she retorted in a shaky whisper as she thrust her legs into the pants and wriggled around to pull them up over her hips. 'You don't have to do anything for me. I can look after myself. I'm well aware that you don't like taking responsibility, at least not that sort of responsibility. That's why you didn't want to get married, isn't it? You were afraid of committing yourself, afraid you might have to consider another person before yourself.'

'Well, well, so you've got the message at last,' he jeered. 'A pity you didn't get it before you decided to choose me as your marriage partner. You made a bad choice, Delia. I'm not the tame house-dog type, but once I was married to you I did try to consider you . . .'

'By going off for months by yourself to some remote place and not keeping in touch,' she muttered as she struggled into her shirt.

'To do a job which I'm trained to do. Te help people in distress who were hurt and diseased,' he said harshly. 'I'd thought, I'd hoped you of all people would have understood. After all, your own father was the same, always going away . . .'

'But he always took my mother with him,' she argued. 'Even after she'd had me she went with him whenever she could.'

'And died of an obscure fever which she picked up in the Congo jungle,' he put in, and she turned sharply to look at him.

'Who told you?' she asked, knowing that she hadn't.

'Marsha, the day we met at her house, before you ever appeared. She was going on about the jungle being an un-suitable place for a woman. She seemed to think it was your father's fault that your mother died,' he said slowly.

'Oh, I know. She hated him. She used to say he'd sacri-ficed my mother to his crazy idealism,' Delia moaned.

'So she said that day, and knowing myself I was deter-mined that no one would ever accuse me of doing the same,' he told her.

Delia stared at the river. The flat water was changing colour as it reflected the fiery reds, glowing oranges and flamingo pinks of a sunset such as she had never seen before.

The whole sky looked as if it were on fire.

'At least my father loved my mother enough to let her choose whether she would go with him or not. You didn't give me that sort of choice,' she replied.

He was sitting so close to her that she felt him stiffen in reaction to her remark.

'Are you implying that I don't love you and have never loved you?' he challenged roughly.

'Yes,' she whispered, and waited hopefully for him to deny the implication.

'Then why are you still married to me?' he demanded, and she guessed that only the presence of other people made him keep his voice low. 'If you believe that why didn't you divorce me? Why the hell are you here, butting into my life again?' His voice shook with the intensity of his feelings. 'God, how I wish you hadn't come!'

It was like receiving a whip-lash across the face and Delia was unable to prevent a cry from escaping her. Fortunately at that moment Mejai, who was in the bow of the boat keeping a look-out, shouted at the same time and everyone looked towards him and not towards her. He was pointing to the bank where a narrow rim of sand curved round a small bay. Jekaro, who was steering, altered the course of the boat until it was pointing towards the crescent of sand.

'I came because Ben sent me,' said Delia stiffly, turning to look at Edmund, glad of her sunglasses because they concealed the tears which had gathered in her eyes. 'And I can't help it if you find my presence here a nuisance. But it won't be for long, and please don't feel you have to be responsible for me. I'll manage very well without your help. I've been managing for some time now.'

She shifted forward and jumped down into the bow of the boat to go and stand beside Mejai. The rich colour of sunset was fading rapidly from the sky and stars were pricking the silvery greyness which took its place. Above the dark trees to the east a huge round yellow moon showed its upper curve.

As Jekaro steered the boat into the bank it became obvious that the bay was bigger than it first appeared from a distance as it was screened from view by an island. In the shelter of the island the water was flat and faintly luminous. Jekaro took the boat as near to the beach as he could and Mejai leapt ashore with a rope in his hand to tie it round a convenient tree so that the boat wouldn't drift away.

They all went ashore in the roughly made Indian canoe which had been towed behind the boat, three of them at a time, taking with them the articles which they would need for the night. Jekaro and Mejai hacked a way through thick undergrowth with sharp, broad-bladed machetes to a small clearing where a dozen small trees made a circle in the centre of which lay a large log, convenient for sitting on.

While the Indians cut wood and made two fires, Luiz, Manoel and Edmund hung the hammocks which had been brought, slinging them between the trees. When the fires were lit Jekaro went back to the boat to fish, Rita told Delia. Interested to see how he would do it, Delia followed him and watched him stand in the stern of the boat to attach a grain of cooked rice to the hook on the end of his line and throw it out into the silvery grey water.

Suddenly the line jerked. The boat rocked as Jekaro balanced himself on the balls of his feet and began to haul the line in. There was a fish on the end of the hook. It was about eight inches long and very plump, and as it leapt about trying to free itself it showed a row of wicked-looking sharp teeth.

'What is it?' Delia asked Edmund, who had come to watch Jekaro too.

'A piranha. How would you like to feel those teeth sinking into your leg? They make very good eating, though, even if they are a little bony.'

He stepped into the canoe, pushed off and let it sidle across the narrow strip of water to the boat, then went aboard and soon appeared beside Jekaro with a fishing line in his hand.

'Perhaps you would like to get some water for cooking in the pans,' said Rita to Delia. 'The way those two are pulling the fish in it looks as if we're going to have a good supper.'

As she dipped a pan into the water Delia noticed for the first time dark log-shapes floating silently in the water, making for the bank. Suddenly one of the shapes zoomed towards her, swept by and out into the bay again. Realising it was a crocodile, she dropped the pan in horror. She groped in the water for the pan, found it and dipped it in again. The shape zoomed in again and she retreated hastily up the bank just as Jekaro and Edmund returned in the canoe with their catch of fish. They rushed past her into the clearing, leaving the fish there, and came running back to the canoe. Edmund was carrying the shotgun.

'What are you going to do?' exclaimed Delia, as he ran past her.

'T·y to shoot that crocodile who fancied a taste of you,' he replied. 'Come and watch.'

Not sure that she wanted to be in the front seat at a killing but realising she must observe all she could if she was to make a success of the articles for the magazine, Delia put her pan of water down and ran after Edmund, leaping into the canoe just as Jekaro pushed off again.

'Here, make yourself useful and shine the torch on the water,' ordered Edmund, thrusting the torch into her hand.

The powerful beam of the flashlight shimmered on the

dark water as the canoe slipped forward slowly. Turning it gradually so that light swept over a wide area, Delia felt Edmund's excitement communicating itself to her, the primitive excitement of the hunt for food, and for the first time she realised how important the hunting of wild animals was to people who lived in the wilderness.

A dark log shape showed up in the beam of light. She saw a reptilian head and two red eyes.

'There he is,' whispered Edmund. 'Keep the light steady on him. His tail will make good eating.'

She heard the click as he released the safety catch on the gun and then the explosion of th shot was in her ears.

'Got him right between the eyes!' Edmund was exultant. But the crocodile was beginning to sink and he had to turn and help paddle the canoe with Jekaro while Delia knelt in the bow still keeping the beam of the torch on the animal.

They reached it just in time. Edmund and Jekaro grabbed the tail and hauled it into the boat. Tail thrashing and wicked-looking teeth snapping, it lay in the bottom while Jekaro, who was grinning with delight, paddled the canoe expertly towards the shore.

There was quite a reception party for the return of the crocodile-hunters. Everyone seemed to be pleased with the catch and congratulated Edmund on his marksmanship. Mejai soon had the tail of the animal cut off and skinned ready for cooking when the supper was ready.

Food for supper was already cooking over the two fires. Rice, onions and tomatoes with a few inches of dried rubbery meat were bubbling in one iron pot and on an improvised barbecue made from green sticks balanced on forked twigs stuck into the ground Mejai was tending the fish which had been caught as they smoked and gave off a delicious smell.

After the excitement of being part of the hunt Delia felt a

little shaky and sat down on the log. At once Edmund shouted at her.

'Don't sit there! It's crawling with ants.'

She got up hastily and shone the torch she was still carrying on to the log. It was crawling with huge black ants.

'They sting,' said Edmund, coming across to her with a spray can of insecticide. 'If you must sit down spray it first. And keep your feet moving all the time. It keeps them away to a certain extent.'

Although still feeling a little huffy after the way he had told her he wished she hadn't come, Delia did as he told her. There was so much for her to learn about living like this. But she could learn as her mother had, and now she was here she was going to show Edmund she could survive in the jungle as well as he could. As far as she could see it was the only way she could prove to him that she loved him and wanted to be with him.

They ate supper quickly, the rice and vegetables with rough spoons and the fish with their fingers. Everyone was sleepy afterwards. Luiz got into his hammock fully dressed and seemed to go to sleep immediately. Manoel and Rita walked off to the edge of the river together, their arms entwined about each other, presumably wishing to be alone for a while before going to bed. Watching them go, Delia felt envy stab her and looked around for Edmund. He wasn't in the clearing. Presumably he wanted to be alone by himself, she thought with a rueful quirk to her mouth. He had managed so long without her company that it wasn't necessary to him now.

There was nothing else to do except get into her hammock, but she felt she couldn't go to bed until she had washed the smell of fish from her hands and the sweat of the day from her body. So she rummaged about until she found her toilet bag and a towel and then walked away from the clearing to the river, going in the opposite direction to that taken by Rita and Manoel.

Shuffling her feet to scare off any snakes, pulling aside creepers which got in her way, she could hear the sinister night sounds of the jungle around her. Birds squawked harshly, an army of insects kept up a persistent hum, crickets chirped and frogs croaked. And there were other sounds too, as if a thousand small animal feet were pattering about.

At last she saw the gleam of moonlight on water. Her fear of the noises was forgotten as she gasped with pleasure at the beauty of the scene before her. Still yellow, the moon laid a path of gold on the placid water and gilded the outlines of huge leaves and glinted on the scimitar curve of a small sandy beach.

Delighted by her find, Delia stepped on to the beach and stripped off her shirt and trousers. She was still wearing her bikini and after a moment's hesitation she stripped that off too, giving in to a longing to immerse herself completely in the cool refreshing water while there was no one there to see her. She would keep her canvas boots on and wouldn't stay in too long.

Carrying her face-cloth and soap in one hand, she stepped into the water. After the heat of the day it felt tepid but wonderfully refreshing. She dipped her face-cloth in and after soaping it began to wash her body. When she was thoroughly soaped all over she stepped further into the water, wading along the shimmering path of moonlight, luxuriating in the feeling of being completely natural. Sinking down until only her head was above the surface, she let the water rinse the soap from her skin, then leapt up, hands above her head as if taking part in some ritual which paid homage to the moon. Twice more she dipped into the water and twice more she jumped up, feeling wonderfully exhilarated.

For a few moments she stood still, face lifted to the moon, her slight breasts taut as if she were offering herself as a living sacrifice, aware of new primitive appetites awakening within her yet feeling a little sad because there was no one with her to share in the beauty of the scene around her.

It was then she felt a nibbling sensation up and down her legs, and looking down, she could see in the clear moonlit water hundreds of tiny fishes, some of which were clinging to her skin like leeches. Waving her legs in a wild can-can dance to get rid of the fish, she made for the shore. Her foot slipped on something unseen and slimy and she fell with a splash. Floundering about, she managed to find her footing again, only to see a long shape, dark and sinister in the moonlight, zooming in towards her.

At once she shrieked, leapt for the shore, slipped again and fell, going right under this time. Coming up, her hair dripping over her face, she went more slowly and felt her heart bump against her ribs when she saw another dark shape standing on the moonlit shore. Someone was watching her.

'Who's there?' she called, and then immediately tried to remember the Portuguese for the question. Neither Jakaro nor Mejai understood English and it could be either of them, come to see what she was doing and possibly to warn her of danger.

'Me. What do you think you're doing?' Edmund sounded wearily exasperated, but the sound of his voice brought relief and she was very glad it was he who was watching her bathe in the nude and not anyone else.

'I was bathing myself and I slipped on something underfoot,' she explained, wading cautiously towards him. Out of the corners of her eyes she saw another log shape come zooming in again and panicked. 'Oh, one of them is after me again!' she cried.

'Here, take my hand,' said Edmund, reaching out. His fingers closed round hers tightly and within seconds she was standing beside him with water dripping off her on to the sand.

'You little fool,' he whispered, still holding her hand. 'Why did you have to strip and go into the river?'

'I felt sticky and dirty. I didn't intend to stay in for long. It was all right until I found the little fish clinging to me.'

'What fish? Where?' he demanded urgently. 'Are you sure they were fish and not leeches?'

'On my legs. Oh no, not leeches, please don't let them be leeches,' she gasped, shaking suddenly from head to foot with something that had nothing to do with fear as she felt the familiar touch of his hands when he smoothed her legs up from the ankles.

'They're all off, now,' he said gruffly, standing up straight. 'I saw you fall in.'

'You saw?' she queried. 'How long have you been here?'

'Long enough to see you bowing to the moon,' he scoffed. 'I saw you leave the clearing and when you were a long time coming back I thought I'd better find out what had happened to you. You should know you shouldn't wander off by yourself in a place like this. And why couldn't you go to bed without bathing for once? Do you have to have all mod. cons. wherever you go?' he added roughly.

'No, I don't,' she mumbled miserably. It seemed that her attempt to prove to him that she could live in the jungle as well as he could was doomed from the start. 'I'm sorry,' she quavered humbly. 'Oh, Edmund . . .' She turned blindly, impulsively towards him, forgetful she wasn't wearing a stitch of clothing, longing to feel the lean hard strength of his body against hers, wanting him with a sudden fierce urgency which made her reckless of what he might think.

He stepped back from her, clicked on the torch he was carrying and shone its beam over the sand until it lit up her heap of clothing. He bent and picked up her shirt.

'Here, put this on,' he ordered curtly, and before she could take it from him he pulled it over her head so roughly that he knocked her off balance. Afraid that she might fall, she clutched at the front of his shirt hearing buttons pop off under the strain.

He dropped the torch and put his hands to her waist to steady her. At once her whole body responded to that familiar and welcome touch and arched against his.

Slowly his hands lost their hardness. His fingers spread out, moving subtly and suggestively, their sensitive tips savouring the smooth dampness of her skin. Up and up they slid under the carelessly draped fold of the shirt. One hand curved about one taut, uplifted breast, the other slid round to the small of her back to press her body more closely against his.

Eagerly her hands fanned out against his chest, exulting in the feel of warm taut skin over hard muscles. Her hands moved up to curve about his throat and round to his nape under the thick curling hair. She lifted her face, her lips parted, her eyes closed.

'This is madness,' he whispered, and her breath came out in a little moan as his open mouth, the lips hard with desire, covered hers.

It was a strange wild coming together; an embrace born of the primitive surroundings; induced by the caress of warm still air on the skin, by the light of the yellow moon, by the deep purple murmuring shadows of the trees.

It ended abruptly. Edmund wrenched himself from her with a muttered expletive and Delia could hear him breathing heavily and shakily. She staggered a little, stepped on something slimy again and slipped, yelped with terror and moved back to him for protection. This time his hands supported her only for a few seconds while she regained her balance, then he snatched them away from her.

'For God's sake,' he rasped between his teeth, 'put that shirt on properly and get your pants on.' He groped on the ground for the torch he had dropped, found it and switched it on again. 'You couldn't have chosen a worse place to turn on. We're both being bitten to death by mosquitoes and there are snakes underfoot.'

Delia realised suddenly that her damp skin had all sorts of insects clinging to it. With shaking hands she brushed them from her and pushed her arms into the sleeves of her shirt. Picking up her pants, she shook them to get rid of ants and pulled them on.

'I wasn't the only one to turn on,' she muttered, pushing her wet hair back from her face. 'You did too,' she accused.

'All right, I admit I did,' he growled in a savage undertone. 'But I'd defy any man with blood in his veins to keep his hands to himself when someone like you, naked in the moonlight, throws herself at him.'

'I didn't throw myself at you,' she protested. 'I . . . I . . . just wanted to . . . to . . . Oh, why are you so unkind and cruel to me?' she cried out.

'In self-defence,' he replied with a curious little laugh. 'I use what weapons I have. Don't make the mistake of believing that what happened just now meant anything. I've no doubt that when you've recovered from your bout of moon-madness you'll be glad I was able to keep control and didn't insist on the usual culmination.'

The taunt was like having the point of a knife touch a sensitive spot in a festering wound. She winced in agony.

'Why? Why do you have to defend yourself against me?' she whispered. 'Oh, Edmund, why can't we be as we used to be when we were first married? We were so happy.'

'Don't you mean you were happy while everything was easy and pleasant?' he remarked dryly. He rubbed at his bare chest with one hand as if it eased a bite which had begun to itch. 'We can't be as we used to be because we've hurt each other too much, I suppose, and it takes time to forgive and forget. Could be neither of us will be able to,' he added sombrely, then slapped viciously at an insect which was biting him and swore. 'This is hardly the place to discuss our relationship,' he went on. 'Let's get back to the clearing and go to bed like everyone else. It'll be another early start in the morning, so you'll need all the sleep you can get. Come on, I'll lead the way with the torch. And go quietly, everyone is asleep.'

Realising that what he said was true and that she was itching already from many bites, Delia groped around for her bikini and toilet bag. They would be covered with ants and other insects and she had lost her face-cloth and soap for ever, but she couldn't throw them away because they were the only ones she had brought with her.

Reaction to what had happened was beginning to set in and it took all her resources of pride to hold back the tears as she stumbled along after Edmund. In the clearing the two fires were crackling merrily, kept alight presumably to keep prowling jungle animals away, and by the orange glow she could see the shapes of the hammocks slung between the trees. All of them were occupied except two on the far side.

'The idea is to get into the hammock and under the mosquito net without an army of mosquitoes getting in with you,' Edmund explained in a cool impersonal whisper. 'I'll spray you with fly spray first to kill any bugs which might be clinging to you.'

'Can't I change into my nightdress?' she asked.

'Do you have it with you?'

'Yes, it's in the hammock under the mosquito net.'

'Okay, you change. You'll probably sleep better if you're out of those clothes. I'll be back in a few minutes to help you get in.'

He went off to the other hammock and standing behind her hammock so that Mejai, who had swung out of his bed to attend to the fires, wouldn't see her she took off her shirt and pants and slipped into the cool cotton nightie. Edmund came back and taking her discarded clothing tied it in a bundle with a piece of string he took from his pants pocket and hung it from the cords which held the hammock to the tree trunk.

'Keep your boots on until you're in and then hand them to me and I'll hang them up in the same way. Never leave any clothing on the ground or it'll be invaded by bugs,' he whispered to her. 'Now, are you ready?'

Delia nodded, and felt his hands warm through the thin stuff of the nightgown as he helped her climb into the hammock, which swayed violently as she burrowed under the netting.

'Lie across it, Brazilian fashion,' he suggested. 'It won't swing so much then. Have you a blanket?'

'Yes, thank you.'

'You'll need it. Sleeping out at night tends to be a chilly and damp business. Goodnight.'

'Goodnight, and thank you,' she replied in a small choked voice as the tears which she had held back gushed suddenly into her eyes.

It wasn't easy to arrange the soft blanket, but after a lot of wriggling she managed to make herself comfortable. Swaying gently, she looked at the glow of the fires, at the other hammocks and then up at the stars winking beyond the dark tracery of branches, through the haze of white cotton which covered her.

How was she going to sleep while her emotions were seesawing so wildly? Out there in the moonlight by the river Edmund had rejected her just as surely as she had rejected him sixteen months ago. *We have both been hurt too much by each other*, he had said, and she realised now that she had hurt him when she had left the flat that evening.

But he could have stopped her from leaving. Why hadn't he? And if only he hadn't gone to see Peter or listened to him. Having been the victim of Peter's suave persuasive charm herself she could understand how easy it must have been for Edmund, humiliated by her apparent rejection of him, to believe everything the smooth-tongued lawyer, his friend for years, had said about her, his young untested wife.

For a while she had found it easy to believe Peter too, when he had told her that she would be better off if she divorced Edmund and that Edmund had come to him and had asked him to make arrangement for a divorce. He had almost persuaded her to agree by using the argument that it was what Edmund wanted when he had made the most surprising mistake.

'When all this is over you'll be free of him and will be able to marry me,' he had said one evening when he had called in to see her.

'But I don't want to marry you,' she had exclaimed. 'I don't want to be married to anyone but Edmund. I . . . I love him and I'll give him his freedom, but that doesn't mean I'll marry you.'

For a few seconds he had looked taken aback. Then he had recovered his polished poise and had come to sit down beside her and had taken her hand in his.

'It's only natural for you to feel like that now,' he had said soothingly. 'After all, it isn't long since Edmund left you. And divorce is always a traumatic experience for a woman, even after such a short marriage as yours has been. I know you're being wrenched apart inside while you're trying to make up your mind, but believe me, you'll feel better once you've made the decision.' He had sighed and added in his worldly-wise way, 'I've seen it happen so many times in my line of business. Edmund has made his decision and there's not a chance in hell of him coming back for a reconciliation. Now it's up to you.'

'Do you have any idea where he is?' Delia had asked hopefully, thinking that personal contact with Edmund might have a happy result.

'Yes, I do, but he asked me not to tell you and I can't betray his confidence even to you,' Peter had replied smoothly. 'I believe he's going on another expedition and could be away for over a year.' He had turned to her earnestly. 'Can't you see, Delia, he's always going to be like that. He's always going to leave you.'

Maybe Aunt Marsha had been right after all, she had thought dully. Edmund was the love-you-and-leave-you type.

'If only I could be sure,' she had muttered. 'Sure that divorce is what he really wants. If only I could talk to him, or even write to him.'

'I'm sure,' said Peter confidently. 'Remember I'm his friend as well as his lawyer. He told me he should never have married you and he wants to rectify the mistake as quickly and as painlessly as possible. He could never bear to see anyone suffer, you know, and he believes you are suffering. Take my advice. Make the decision for your own sake, for your own peace of mind.'

But she hadn't made it because she had begun to be aware of changes in her body. She had counted up weeks and found that three months had passed by since Edmund had been home between his two periods of absence first in Indonesia and then in Central America and that there was a possibility she was pregnant. A visit to a doctor had confirmed her suspicion that she was carrying Edmund's child and the idea of divorce had gone right out of her head.

The hammock swung crazily as Delia wriggled around in it trying to burrow more snugly into the blanket, wishing she had the sleeping pills Edmund had taken from her. What would he have said if she had told him that the illness from which she had suffered had been a nervous breakdown after she had lost the child and that the pills had been prescribed for moments like this when she couldn't bear to think about what had happened?

But now, in this tented airborne bed, in the firelit clearing in the jungle she was having to think about it, face up to it, and suddenly she was wishing that she was back in the hot shuttered room in Posto Orlando. There, with Edmund lying on the other bed, she could have whispered to him in the darkness and shared with him at last the experience of those first months after he had left her. Talking to him would have relieved the ache of regret and eased a little the deep sense of loss and disappointment because the baby boy had been born prematurely and had died soon after birth.

For she had been glad when she had discovered she was carrying Edmund's child and she had tried hard to find out where he had gone so that she could tell him. Distrusting Peter, she hadn't told him, although she had asked him again if he would tell her where Edmund was. He had been very bland, had shrugged his shoulders and had said, 'Your guess is as good as mine.' And after that she had gone out of her way to avoid meeting him.

She had gone to the Red Cross headquarters thinking Edmund might be doing voluntary work for them. They had no idea where he was. She had gone to the research institute where he had once worked and they had given her an address which she hadn't known about before, the address of his great-uncle. So she had written to Edmund care of it. A week or so later her letter had been returned with a covering letter from Justin Talbot, who said he was surprised to learn that his great-nephew Edmund was married but that he had no idea of Edmund's whereabouts.

Delia fell asleep suddenly, overwhelmed by emotional exhaustion. She awoke to find everyone else was up and moving about in the pearly misty light of dawn. Casting off the mosquito net, she reached for the bundle of clothes and taking them under the netting with her began to dress, the hammock swaying wildly as she wriggled.

There was nothing much left for breakfast, only a cup of tepid coffee and some cold fish and rice. Although her stomach turned over at the sight of the food she ate it, realising she would be very hungry later if she didn't. Then following the example of the others she carried all the articles she had taken ashore back to the boat and soon it was chugging peacefully downstream.

Delia sat in the bows with Luiz, her notebook on her knee, occasionally making notes while he told her about his work with the tribes and of his struggle to give them the confidence to deal with the modern world which was slowly but inexorably encroaching on their way of life.

'I provide them with implements which will be of use to them—steel axes and knives instead of stone ones, guns for hunting, fishing tackle. Food and clothing only when they ask for them,' he said. 'Too often in the past these people have been demoralised and denigrated by the white people who have forced their ways, their religion and culture on a people who have their own religions and their own culture. Now I encourage them to keep their tribal customs, the dances and the rituals, the arts and crafts.'

His sincerity showed in every word, every gesture, and she could not help but admire him. They talked all morning. He mentioned her father and how much he had helped the tribes by publicising them through his articles and lectures. And he talked of Edmund.

'I would like to think he'll come back here and work for us,' he said. 'Has he spoken to you about it yet?'

'No, not yet,' she said.

'It will not be an easy decision for him to make, I realise that now that I have met you.' His dark eyes twinkled roguishly. 'When a man is a bachelor like myself he does not have such problems to deal with. I hope you and he will come to some compromise as Manoel and Rita have done. They tell me that is what marriage is all about—loving each other enough to reach a compromise.'

As on the previous day the heat and glare on the water became almost unbearable and Delia was glad to take shelter in the engine house in spite of the fumes. Curling up against the pieces of baggage, she alternately dozed and wrote busily. For a while Rita joined her to talk, but Edmund kept aloof from her, staying outside on the roof and sometimes helping to steer the boat.

Half way through the afternoon they were caught in a shower of heavy rain which swished through the jungle and across the river like a thick grey curtain, blotting out the views and soaking everything which was in its way. The rain had barely stopped when the boat turned a wide bend in the river and pointed towards a cluster of wooden huts scattered about an emerald green bank in a jungle clearing. It was so unusual among the seemingly never-ending dark forest that seeing it was like coming across a tiny unflawed diamond among a clutter of semi-precious stones. It was Binauros.

Contrarily the strong current which had carried them down river now seemed determined to sweep them past the village. Jekaro and Mejai needed the help of Edmund and Manoel to fight the current with long poles and turn the boat towards the bank. At last they were near enough for Mejai to throw the rope ashore. It was caught by a tall Indian who was standing on the bank and who pulled the boat alongside a small wooden jetty.

A group of Indians, most of them dressed in shorts and shirts, stood on the bank, strangely silent. Suddenly the air was split by a high-pitched wailing noise and a woman appeared. She was wearing a shapeless cotton dress and was screaming and beating her breast while tears flowed down her cheeks from glassy staring eyes.

Jekaro moved forward and jumped ashore. At once the woman stopped crying, grasped him by the arm. Grinning with embarrassment, Jekaro allowed her to drag him up the slope towards the huts. And then the group of silent Indians began to shout and laugh. They rushed on to the boat to greet Luiz, touching him with reverence, shaking his hands and putting their arms about him before turning to do the same to Manoel.

'What was all that about?' Delia asked Rita.

'The woman is the mother of Jekaro. She was crying for all the days he has been away from this village. Everyone had to remain silent until she had performed the ritual of welcoming him. Shall we go ashore? The welcoming party will carry our luggage to the huts.'

Delia was glad to step off the boat, but instead of being firm the ground seemed to heave under her feet as if she was still on the boat. She staggered a little out of control and might have fallen if her arm hadn't been grasped. A man spoke to her laughingly in Portuguese and she looked up to find she was being supported by a slim handsome Brazilian of about thirty years of age who was dressed in a crisp white shirt and white trousers.

His dark brown eyes gleamed with admiration as he smiled down at her, but she couldn't understand a word he was saying. By concentrating hard she managed to remember enough Portuguese to thank him, and at once his face lit up with understanding.

'It was my pleasure,' he said in heavily-accented English.

'Ah, Carlo. I did not expect to find you here.' Luiz with the group of Indians following him had come ashore and he and the younger man exchanged the *abraço*. 'I see that you are as chivalrous as ever,' he went on in English so that Delia could understand. 'This is Delia Talbot, a journalist who is here with us to collect information for articles. Delia, I would like you to meet Carlo Silveira, son of one of our great explorers and one of the pilots who serve the protection service so well.'

'Talbot?' queried Carlo as he shook Delia's hand. 'Any relation to Dr Talbot?'

'She is his wife,' Luiz flung over his shoulder as he went off up the slope towards the huts.

'Is this true?' exclaimed Carlo. 'How long have you been married to Edmund?'

'Two and a half years,' Delia replied as they began to walk after Luiz.

'Incredible!' he exclaimed again. 'I had no idea. I have flown Edmund to many different places during the past twelve months, and not once did he tell me he was married.'

A woman was coming down the path towards them. She was tall and slim and was dressed in pale beige cotton slacks and a matching shirt. Delia judged her to be a few years older than herself, about twenty-six. She had smooth black hair and the same lovely copper-tinted tan possessed by Rita. Stepping in front of them, she spoke curtly to Carlo in Portuguese, making a gesture towards Delia with one hand. He answered in the same language, his mouth curving on a faintly sardonic smile as he mentioned Delia's name. The woman's face stiffened and her dark long-lashed eyes widened as she turned to Delia.

'I did not know Edmund had a wife,' she said in slow careful English. 'I am Dr Zanetta Mireilles. I looked after Edmund when he had malaria after being lost in the jungle.'

'*Bom dia*, doctor. I'm pleased to meet you,' said Delia, offering her hand. But Zanetta had looked past her and with a muttered excuse, hurried down the slope. Turning, Delia watched her go.

Edmund was coming up the slope carrying his bag from the boat. Zanetta ran up to him. He stopped, smiled at her and said something. In answer the Brazilian woman flung her arms around him in the *abraço*, kissing him on both cheeks not once but three times, until, laughing, he dropped the bag and returned the embrace.

Delia turned sharply on her heel, and encountered Carlo's glinting black eyes. He seemed to be very amused by what had just happened, but he said nothing and together they walked on to the clearing.

'You and Edmund will share a hut with Manoel and Rita,' explained Luiz. 'Here we do not have the same amenities as at Posto Orlando. We sleep in hammocks and if you want a shower there is one in that hut in the centre of the compound.'

He took her to the hut. It was built on stilts and a flight of wooden steps led up to a waist-high doorway. Inside was a big airy room. Only one end and one side of the room were walled up to the roof. The other end and side had half walls and were open above them to the weather like a verandah. A kerosene lamp made from a cotton wick stuck in a tin can was attached to one of the tree trunks which supported the roof of plaited palm fronds and by its flickering smoky light two Indians were slinging the hammocks they had carried up from the boat, two at one end of the room.

As soon as they saw Delia they came over to her and pointed to her bag. Recognising the signs, she found sweets and cigarettes for them and they left the hut with Luiz. Rita and Manoel came in and went to their end of the hut while Delia changed her soiled creased shirt for a clean close-fitting cotton sweater, brushed her hair and wondered where Edmund was.

The moon was large and yellow and the air was heavy with the scent of limes as she walked a little later with Rita and Manoel to the eating house, which was close to the river. On the way in they passed the kitchen and she noticed a fire flickering on a raised platform flanked by a clay baking oven, where an elderly Indian was supervising the cooking of chunks of golden juicy meat.

'We're going to eat well again tonight,' said Rita. 'The hunters of the tribe were lucky today. They found a herd of wild boar and killed many of them.'

In the long room where they were to eat some of the hunters were sitting around Luiz describing to him with a great deal of mime how they had stalked and killed the boars. At the long table Edmund was sitting next to Zanetta Mireilles.

'Has anyone introduced you to Dr Mireilles?' Rita whispered to Delia as they took their seats on a bench on the other side of the table.

'Yes, Carlo did. She seems very young to be a doctor. Is she a volunteer?'

'Yes, from the São Paulo school of medicine. She wishes to specialise in tropical medicine. She comes from a very wealthy family.'

Like Edmund does, thought Delia miserably, wondering what else he had in common with the attractive, vivacious woman doctor.

'I hope you do not mind me telling you this, Delia,' said Rita, leaning closer. 'I do so out of the friendship I feel for you even though we have not known each other long. I think Zanetta became very fond of Edmund while she was at Posto Orlando and he was ill.'

And did he become fond of her? The question leapt up in Delia's mind, but she didn't ask it because she didn't want to embarrass Rita.

She glanced surreptitiously across the table. Edmund was sitting with his arms folded on the table. His eyes were hidden by their heavy lids and his face was wreathed in smoke from the cigarette he was smoking, but she could see he was smiling slightly as he listened to Zanetta, who was talking to him urgently with many gestures of her small slim hands.

Doctors' talk? Delia wondered. How would she ever know what was being said? How would she ever know what Edmund was thinking or if he was listening? Was he pretending to listen as he had once pretended to listen to Aunt Marsha?

Zanetta paused, looking at him expectantly. He answered at once in his fairly fluent Portuguese. She spoke again and he answered. They were engrossed in their conversation, not knowing and perhaps not caring about what was going on around them.

Jealousy rose in a green tide to swamp Delia. All day Edmund had ignored her on the boat, but this evening he could give his undivided attention to this Brazilian doctor who had greeted him as if he were her lover.

Blindly Delia turned, and found Carlo sitting on her right. She smiled at him and he smiled back, his very dark eyes crinkling at the corners.

'I am still in a state of surprise,' he confessed. 'How could Edmund come here and spend so much time here without you? He must be a little—how do you say it? Crazy in the head?' he touched his temple with his forefinger and rolled his eyes. 'Only a mad man would leave a wife as pretty as you behind for some other man to steal from him while his back is turned. And why did you let him come?'

'I couldn't stop him,' she replied.

'No? I cannot believe that. I am sure if you put your mind to it you could prevent any man from leaving you. Or are you going to tell me it is one of those modern marriages where you go your separate ways, meeting only occasionally when neither of you is too busy at your work?'

'You sound as if you don't think much of such marriages,' she parried.

'No, I don't. If I were married, which I have no intention of being just yet,' he said with his charming smile, 'I would like my wife to stay at home, look after me, the house and the children when they come.'

'But supposing you aren't there to look after? Supposing you have to go away all the time?'

'I would expect her to wait for me, be faithful to me, welcome me with open arms when I return.' He glanced across the table at Zanetta and Edmund, and leaned towards

Delia until his dark head was just touching hers and with a hand to his mouth he whispered behind it, 'I do not care for cold women such as that one over there. Always she is talking about herself, how clever she is as a doctor—yap, yap, yap! With all that talk there is no time for kissing.'

Delia couldn't help laughing, and as they ate the tender sweet wild boar meat which had a crisp crackling and was flavoured with wood-smoke she was glad she was sitting by Carlo, for he told her amusing and sometimes hair-raising tales about his flying career in the jungle, diverting her attention from Edmund and Zanetta and making her forget her worries.

When the meal was over they went outside to sit on benches in front of the eating house and watch Indians dance, wearing feathered headdresses, and carrying spears. It was a dance of anger, Carlo told her, because they were upset about the new road which was being cut through the jungle and which would disrupt the way of life of some of the tribes. Several times during the course of the dance the warriors rushed, spears at the ready, as if about to attack the small group of white people watching them. They were expressing their determination to fight against the coming of the road.

As a breeze rustled the leaves and large bats flew across the yellow disc of the moon Delia walked to the hut, escorted by Carlo. The air was cool and smelt of damp earth as well as lime blossom, and the romantic surroundings must have stirred Carlo's blood, for at the bottom of the flight of steps he took Delia's hand in his and lifted it to his lips.

'Goodnight, Delia. I am glad you have come here and shall look forward to seeing you tomorrow,' he whispered, and turning away, walked off into the darkness.

In the hut the kerosene lamp still flickered making black

shadows dance along the walls. Delia undressed, put on her nightdress and managed to get into the hammock and under the netting without help. Swinging gently, hearing the murmur of Rita's and Manoel's voices as they talked at the other end of the hut, she closed her eyes, although she knew she wouldn't sleep until Edmund came.

He came at last and she heard him moving quietly as he undressed and swung into his hammock. Wishing for courage to break the silence and speak to him to ask him where he had been and what he had been doing, she opened her eyes again. The room was in darkness. He had put out the lamp and the smell of the smoke tickled her nose.

She was closer to him in the night, yet she had never felt so far from him. The gulf separating them seemed to be growing wider and wider and she was sure that she had discovered why he wanted to stay in Brazil. He wanted to be with Dr Zanetta Mireilles.

CHAPTER FIVE

'There's a very sick man in one of the more isolated villages in the middle of the jungle. The tribe has sent a message asking for a doctor to go and look at him. Carlo says he'll fly me there this morning. Would you like to come?'

Edmund spoke coolly and Delia, who had only just rolled out of her hammock and was searching for a towel and some soap to take to the shower hut with her, stood still for a moment, her back to him, hardly able to believe her ears. He had asked her to go somewhere with him!

Turning, she looked at him curiously. He had obviously showered or had been for a swim, because his hair was damp, coiling close to his head in flat ringlets and cork-screwing about his ears and neck. Freshly shaved, his face looked bronzed and healthy after the two days on the river and his blue eyes gleamed with life, but the shadows under them and in the hollows of his cheeks told their own tale. He hadn't slept well last night.

'Would you like me to come?' she asked hesitantly yet hopefully.

'What do you want me to say?' he retorted with a touch of exasperation. 'I ask you a simple question and you answer with another. Carlo says the plane will take four of us. Luiz says it will be interesting for you to visit this particular village. The opportunity is there. You take it or you don't. It's up to you.'

His sharpness pricked, and Delia swallowed hard. She had woken with a sick headache and had pains in her stomach.

She would have given anything to have rolled herself into the hammock again to sleep off the feeling of illness, but she also wanted to be with him and prove to him that she could go anywhere that he went.

'I . . . I'd like to come with you, please,' she said quickly. 'Who is the fourth person?'

'Dr Mireilles. It will be good experience for her too,' he replied curtly. 'Okay, I'll go and tell Carlos you'll be with us. If you have any presents left which you can give to the villagers bring them with you. I'll see you at the eating house in about fifteen minutes, then.'

He turned away and left the hut before she could ask him a question concerning his own welfare. How did he feel about going up in a small aircraft after being so recently in a crash? Did he feel nervous? And if he did would he ever admit to it?

She pulled on the inevitable shirt and pants and hurried to the shower hut. Inside there was a place to leave her clothing and a small cubicle with a half door. Over the cubicle was a tank and when she pulled on a rope it tipped warm rain water over her. Although a rather violent way in which to shower it was refreshing and washed away the feeling of nausea, so that she was able to eat some of the excellent breakfast provided by the Indian cook. There were fried eggs, produced, Luiz told her, by the free-ranging hens kept by the tribe, and light golden pancakes made from maize flour.

Carlo greeted her with warmth and seemed delighted that she was going on the flight. With his arm through hers he marched her off to the airstrip where the small plane was parked, its red and white paint gleaming in the misty morning sunlight. He was wearing sand-coloured trousers tucked into a pair of scuffed flying boots and a pale pink shirt. Round his waist he wore a broad leather belt with a holster into which was tucked a businesslike revolver. In his other hand he carried a rifle.

'I take them as a precaution,' he explained to her as he helped her up into the cockpit of the plane. 'If I have to land somewhere in the jungle I'm well equipped for hunting my own food. Now I'd like you to sit in front with me. You will be more comfortable there and will see more. Also I shall enjoy your company.'

Zanetta and Edmund arrived accompanied by Luiz and a group of Indians. As he climbed up into the cockpit Edmund frowned at Delia.

'Why are you sitting in front?' he asked.

'Because I asked her to, my friend,' replied Carlo with his wide smile. 'Do not worry, she will be quite safe with me. You may sit at the back and talk shop with the other doctor.'

Edmund flicked a glance in the direction of Zanetta, who was already in her seat, then lifted his shoulder in a shrug.

'Okay,' he said, 'just as you like.' And he moved past to take his seat.

The door was closed. The engine sputtered into life. Delia fastened her seat belt and the plane bumped across the grass on to the runway. It gathered speed and lifted smoothly off the ground. Looking down, Delia waved to Luiz and the Indians and then to Rita and Manoel as the plane flew low over the village clearing.

Carlo flew the plane as if he were a part of it. Like a bird gliding on a current of air they drifted low over the river to see crocodiles, dark and sinister-looking, basking on sandbanks, they circled over a patch of savannah where a herd of deer was drinking by a clump of twisted trees. Banking away from the clearing, they sidled above thick trees, a continuous sea of dark green broken only by the silvery gleam of a river or a dark muddy swamp. Just below them flocks of long-tailed macaws flew too, flashes of brilliant red and blue against the sombre greens.

'How will you find the village?' asked Delia, raising her voice against the noise of the engine and leaning close to Carlo so he would hear her. His dark eyes smiled at her when he turned his head to look at her.

'It is a mystery which I have to solve,' he said. 'The jungle is like a maze. First we go this way and then we go that, always with an eye on the compass until we see at last a curl of smoke coming up through the trees, and where there is smoke there is life.' He leaned a little closer to her so he could lower his voice. 'This is Edmund's first flight in a small plane since the crash. I would like to know how he is reacting.'

He straightened up and paid attention to his flying once more. Cautiously Delia looked over her shoulder into the back seats of the plane. Edmund wasn't talking to Zanetta and since she wasn't talking either but was staring sullenly out of the window beside her he wasn't listening to her. He wasn't looking out of the window on his side. He was staring straight ahead and the expression in his narrowed eyes as they met her wary glance made Delia feel a little uneasy. They seemed to be blazing with anger.

She turned back and settled herself in her seat. Very much aware that Edmund was still staring at her, she didn't lean towards Carlo but waited until he leaned towards her.

'How is he?' he asked.

'He seems all right.'

'Good. I'm glad. I would not have liked him to have lost his nerve. Look down over there. Do you see smoke? That is our village.'

The little plane seemed to fall downwards. A clearing in

the dense green appeared. Carlo circled over the straw-roofed huts and several Indians ran out waving and shouting.

As the plane curved round and flew directly into the sun Delia looked down. Indians were running in one direction along a path which had been hacked through the trees. Even women and children were running and some of the smaller children fell over and were snatched up from the ground by their mothers in the rush to the airstrip.

The runway was very short and Carlo had to turn the plane again to make his approach. It skimmed just above the tops of tall trees, making the smaller branches toss with the wind of its passage and hit the ground with a bump, the brakes squealed as Carlo hauled it to a stop with its propeller almost touching the nearest hut in the village.

As soon as the door was opened large brown hands reached in to help Carlo out. Delia, Edmund and Zanetta were helped down in the same way and soon were being led at a fast sweat-breaking trot through the thick humid heat to the centre of the village. There was no doubt the villagers were very upset about something. They waved their hands, rolled their eyes and shouted all the time.

'What are they yelling about?' demanded Edmund, coming to a stop at the edge of the clearing, and everyone stopped with him. 'I'm not going any further until I know.'

Heat rose from the beaten and baked earth like a blast from an oven set at roasting temperature. Feeling slightly giddy, Delia swayed a little on her feet and the huts and the faces of the people crowding around Edmund seemed to blur before her eyes. Carlo was listening to an explanation which was being made by a big muscular teak-skinned man who was dressed in rather ragged shirt and shorts and who spoke a rough broken Portuguese.

'They are glad we have come,' Carlo said at last to

Edmund. 'This is the chief and he wants you to go to the sick man straight away.'

'Where is he?' asked Edmund.

'In the hut on the other side of the clearing. You go ahead with him,' suggested Carlo.

'I can't understand much of what he says,' Edmund said. 'I'll have to have an interpreter.'

'Dr Mireilles is most willing to do that for you, I'm sure,' said Carlo with a sardonic twist to his mouth. 'Won't you, Zanetta?' he added, turning to the woman doctor and speaking to her in Portuguese.

'But of course,' she answered with a supercilious lift of her eyebrows.

Edmund's blue glance swerved to Delia. Knowing how observant he was, she hoped she looked well, even though her head was pounding and her stomach was churning.

'Will you be all right?' he asked softly, and she felt hope leap alive within her. If he cared so much about her welfare surely he could be made to care for her again in other ways.

'I'll be fine, thank you. Maybe I'll take some photographs,' she said, smiling in an effort to show she was well.

'Don't worry,' said Carlo smoothly. 'I shall look after Delia and show her round the village.'

Edmund gave him a strange narrow-eyed glance, then nodded.

'All right,' he agreed. 'I'll be as quick as I can.'

He turned to the chief and said something in Portuguese. The chief patted him on the shoulder, then took him by the arm and led him across the clearing to a hut from which the sound of harsh wailing was coming.

Carlo spoke abruptly and coldly to Zanetta, who hadn't moved. The woman gave him a furious glance, spat a few words at him and then marched off towards the hut into which Edmund had disappeared, clutching her black doctor's bag in her hand.

'We shall wait for a few minutes, here on this bench in the shade,' said Carlo, and with his hand beneath Delia's elbow he guided her over to a big tree which had been left standing in the middle of the clearing. They sat on a rough bench made from a tree log and Indians crowded around them to stare curiously. Remembering her presents, Delia opened the satchel handbag and brought out packets of toffees and cigarettes to offer them round.

This tribe was different again from the others she had met. Their skin was teak-coloured and many of them were very thickly painted. All the men wore armbands of spotted jaguar skin. They pushed forward to touch her, taking hold of her arms, and her hair, lifting her hand to examine her wedding ring and fingering the gold chain and medallion which she wore around her neck. She sat patiently, knowing now how important this physical contact was to them. She smiled at them and they smiled back shyly.

Then one of the women issued a sharp order, and a youth ran off to a hut and came back with a handful of nuts to offer them to her. They were soft and sticky. Not liking to show that her stomach was heaving at the sight of them, Delia pressed the nuts in her mouth. They were acid to taste and mouth-drying.

'They like you,' murmured Carlo. 'And that is a good sign, for this tribe is very shy. It is also one of the more creative tribes, as you will see later. *God!*' he exclaimed, rising suddenly to his feet. 'She is out already.'

Delia looked across the clearing. Zanetta was running away from the hut. Carlo went across to intercept her, speaking to her sharply. Zanetta, whose face looked greenish yellow and whose dark eyes were black and staring, answered wildly and turning on her heel with her hand clasped to her mouth ran off behind another hut.

'What is the matter with her?' exclaimed Delia, going over to Carlo.

'She did not like what she saw in there,' he replied with a twist to his mouth. 'Ah, what good is she if she is sick to her stomach when she sees someone who is ill? She should not be a doctor out here in the jungle. She is not dedicated enough, not in the way that Edmund is.' He slanted a glance at Delia. 'You know, I have come to admire him very much. At first I did not like him.' He lifted his shoulders and made an expressive repudiating gesture with his hands. 'I looked at his curly hair, his cold blue eyes, and listened to his soft voice, and I thought, here is just another blasé rich boy, tired of his sophisticated way of life, coming to the jungle for kicks. But after a while I changed my mind. He is a fine man who is concerned about other people and wants to help them. And he is tough, all the way through. To have survived the way he did when he was lost he had to be.'

'He's at the door of the hut,' said Delia. 'He's beckoning to us.'

They walked across the bright clearing to the hut where Edmund was standing. He looked rather pale and sweat was beading his brow, but his eyes and voice were steady.

'Where's Dr Mireilles?' he asked sharply.

'Being sick behind a bush,' sneered Carlo. 'Do you need help?'

'Yes—with the language. I can't make head or tail what they're saying about the boy in there. Something to do with a bird. Delia, you're not to come in.'

'I want to,' she insisted, looking him in the eye.

'It isn't very pleasant.'

'Illness rarely is,' she retorted. 'I want to see inside the hut, for copy, for my articles,' she added appealingly.

'Okay,' he said resignedly. 'Come in.'

Inside was dark and the darkness was full of a harsh crying sound. At last she was able to make out a group of women crouched around a hammock. They were rocking backwards and forwards as they wailed. In the hammock was a small figure which Delia thought was a child, but when she looked more closely she felt chilled as she saw black eyes staring out of a face which had once been a man's but had shrunk to the size of a child's.

'What's happened?' she gasped.

The chief was speaking, using his hands to imitate time, sleep and hunting, and Carlo translated slowly in terse sentences.

'He is a young man. He went hunting. He lost his weapons. He went to look for water. He lost his way in the jungle. He had no food, no water, so the Ananu bird took him up into the tree tops. Yesterday the Ananu brought him back to the village.'

'What is this Ananu bird?' Edmund whispered, his gaze still on the figure in the hammock.

'When an Indian is lost in the jungle the tribe believes that a beast, half man and half bird, takes him up to its nest and keeps him there. When the Ananu gets bored with him it picks him up in its beak and takes him back to his people.'

'I see. A myth to explain what is inexplicable to the tribe,' muttered Edmund. 'He is of course suffering from severe malnutrition and dehydration. We have to get him to Posto Orlando at once if his life is to be saved.' He turned to Carlo with a grin. 'You're going to be the Ananu which takes him away again but brings him back restored to health.'

'That is a good suggestion of yours, my friend,' replied Carlo, grinning back. 'But I cannot take him to Posto

Orlando in that plane with the four of us up as well. It will be too much weight. She is not young, that plane of mine, and the runway is too short here for me to get her off with an extra load.' He made an expressive gesture with one hand. 'It would be very touch and go and I would not like to crash it.'

'But that fellow in there hardly weighs anything at all,' protested Edmund.

'I realise that, but you see the chief, his brother, will want to come too, and his mother. They won't let him go alone. After your time with the tribes you must know how they cling to each other, especially in time of illness. And I'd put the chief's weight at about a hundred and fifty kilos,' said Carlo.

Edmund stared at him, his eyes narrowed in thought, then wiped the sweat of his forehead on his forearm.

'*Faugh!*' he exclaimed with a grimace of disgust. 'Let's get out of this place and discuss it outside. I wonder if we could have something to drink?'

Carlos spoke to the chieftain, who nodded and came outside with them. Zanetta had reappeared and was sitting on the bench under the tree. Edmund went straight to her, sat down beside her and spoke to her gently. Watching, Delia felt jealousy stir in her. She sat on the end of the bench with her back to them.

Directed by the chief, some women came forward shyly and offered them juicy fresh passion-fruit. They took them eagerly and for a while didn't speak as they sucked the pinkish-orange thirst-quenching flesh of the fruit.

'Two of us will have to stay behind,' said Edmund suddenly and authoritatively. 'Only you can fly the plane, Carlo, so you will have to go. It's a case of deciding who will stay.'

'The two women or you and one of them,' said Carlo.

There was a brief silence broken only by the sounds of them eating more fruit and the squawking of macaws and parakeets. Delia decided that the two men were waiting for herself or Zanetta to make some sort of offer.

'I don't mind staying behind,' she said quietly. 'It will be good copy for my articles.'

'Then I'll stay with you,' said Edmund promptly.

At once Zanetta broke into a torrent of speech. Her eyes flashing and her hands gesturing wildly, she was obviously worked up about something.

'What's the matter with her now?' Delia whispered to Carlo, who was sitting beside her.

'She wants you to go in the plane with me and says she'll stay behind with Edmund. What a fool that woman is,' replied Carlo dryly.

'Oh, tell her I'll go with you and she can stay,' muttered Delia miserably. 'It makes no difference.'

'I'll do nothing of the sort,' retorted Carlo. 'It is for Edmund to decide.' He turned away and spoke rather viciously to Zanetta in Portuguese, presumably telling her to be quiet. Then he said to Edmund, 'It is up to you, my friend. Perhaps it would be easier if you came with me and left the two women here.' His voice lilted a little with mockery at such an idea.

'No. It will be best if I stay,' replied Edmund coolly. 'I'm the heaviest. Zanetta will go with you because the patient must have someone medical with him on the flight to give him an injection if necessary.'

'And who is going to tell Zanetta that?' asked Carlo, still mocking.

'I will. She'll do what I tell her because I'm the senior doctor,' replied Edmund imperturbably. 'Do you think you'll be able to come back here before nightfall to pick Delia and me up?'

'I doubt it. It would be best if you assume I won't be back until tomorrow. I'll speak to the chief and arrange for you to stay the night here,' said Carlo, rising to his feet.

'Then that's all settled,' said Edmund. 'All we have to do is get the boy from the hut to the plane and make him comfortable. You might ask the chief to make some form of rough stretcher to carry the patient from here to the airstrip.'

'Okay!' Carlo went off to the hut where the sick man was and Edmund turned to Zanetta and began to talk to her quietly in Portuguese.

Wishing she could understand what he was saying, Delia sat hunched at the end of the bench and watched some skinny Indian children playing a rough sort of baseball, wondering where they found the energy to run about in the midday heat. And slowly she began to see the funny side of the situation. Here was Edmund having to explain to the fierce and obviously very possessive Zanetta why it was necessary for her to go in the plane while he stayed behind with *his wife*.

Carlo came back with the chief, the chief's wife and a man who was introduced as his brother and who was a headman of the tribe.

'It is agreed that you both stay the night here,' explained Carlo. 'They have a hut arranged specially for guests and since you are friends of their great friend Luiz Santos they are pleased to have you stay the night with them. Now we go to make the stretcher from some poles cut from trees and a spare hammock.'

'Good.' Edmund stood up, and thinking she might be of some help Delia rose to her feet too. At once he turned to her. 'You stay here in the shade,' he said curtly.

'Can't I help?' she asked, looking up at him.

He stared at her, his eyes hard and bright under the shade of the brim of the old straw hat. He raised a hand, reached out as if to touch her face, then withdrew it sharply and turned on his heel away from her.

'Not right now,' he muttered over his shoulder, and walked off after Carlo and the chief.

Delia sank down on the bench. At the other end of it Zanetta sat in sullen silence watching Edmund go across the clearing. Suddenly she stood up, stepped sideways and plonked herself down beside Delia.

'Why did you have to come here to Brazil?' she said in her gutturally accented English. 'Why did you have to follow Edmund here?'

'I didn't follow him,' Delia said sharply and protestingly, then broke off. This was one time when she was going to be honest about her reason for coming to Brazil. 'I came to be with Edmund because I'm his wife and I love him,' she said quietly, looking Zanetta in the eyes.

The dark eyes widened briefly, then narrowed with scorn. The pretty full-lipped passionate mouth curved in a sneer, as Zanetta looked away across at the hut where the sick man lay.

'He does not love you,' she said, speaking slowly and with emphasis. 'If he did he would have told us about you. He would have talked about you, but the only time he did talk was when he was delirious with fever. Several times he moaned about someone called Delia.' Zanetta shrugged her shoulders. 'As you must know, the subconscious mind behaves peculiarly when one is feverish. It was mostly rubbish he talked, but there were these two names over and over— Delia and Peter. I had the impression Peter was your lover.' She sighed. 'Poor Edmund, he was very ill,' she added. 'If I had not nursed him he would have died.'

Delia's hands clenched on her knees. Everything before her, the straw-roofed huts, the dark jungle trees crowding beyond them, seemed rimmed with red as a fury such as she had never known blazed up within her so that she had a longing to turn and strike the Brazilian woman who was sitting beside her, scratch at her face, pull her hair, destroy her. She shook with the force of the primitive feeling of furious jealousy because this woman had done for Edmund what she was supposed to do. She had cared for him when he had been ill.

The feeling passed suddenly, leaving her exhausted and subdued. Her throat was dry and she longed for more passion-fruit to ease it, and her head throbbed painfully.

'I'm grateful,' she mumbled, 'glad that you were able to nurse him and make him better.'

'Ha!' Zanetta's laugh was a tinkle of mockery. 'I did not do it for *you* but for *me*. I had met him twice before, once in Rio where we walked beside the surf under the stars when he visited my parents' home in Ipanema and then later in Brasilia. It is because I admire him so much that I volunteered to come out to Binauros to work for the protection service. I hoped I would meet him again, and I did. I love him much more than you do and he loves me. That is why I should be staying here with him tonight and not you.'

'You can stay, for all I care,' cried Delia, getting to her feet, 'but don't expect me to leave. I'm staying too because I have a right to be with Edmund. You haven't.'

Although she realised she was going against Edmund's orders by moving out of the shade she walked away, unable to bear Zanetta's company any longer. Through the thick hazy heat she walked, not really noticing where she was going as Zanetta's words beat in her brain like the blows of a hammer. *I love him more than you do and he loves me.*

It could be true, then, what she had suspected, and Zanetta was the reason why Edmund wanted to stay in Brazil. And was it really surprising? They had so much in common and Zanetta had saved his life when he was ill.

Delia groaned as she stumbled along a narrow path which twisted between tall trees festooned with creepers with huge flat leaves shimmering in shafts of sunlight. Beside her a troop of monkeys swung from branch to branch, chattering cheekily and occasionally letting out heart-freezing howls.

Sweat poured down her back and legs. Her head throbbed and she had no idea where she was going. But did it matter? Did anything matter if Edmund was in love with someone else? If he was it explained everything which had happened since she had come; his rejection of her, his attempt to have her sent back to Brasilia, his violent repudiation of the way they had kissed the other night, his cool aloof behaviour since then.

Not looking where she was going, she tripped over an exposed tree root and fell headlong. At once, or so it seemed, there were a dozen hands laid on her to help her to her feet. Standing once more, she found she was surrounded by several young women, some completely bare, the others dressed in shapeless cotton shifts, all with dark curtains of hair half covering their faces and all staring at her with dark anxious eyes. One of them, who seemed slightly older than the others, touched her on the arm and then pointed through the trees, and looking in that direction, Delia saw the shimmer of sunlight on the water. She looked enquiringly at the woman.

The woman made movements with her arms as if she were swimming, then pointed at Delia and then at the water again. It seemed as if she was asking Delia if she would like to go swimming. To make sure Delia pointed at herself, pointed at the water and made swimming movements with her arms too. The woman grinned, showing that she had several teeth missing, and nodded. Delia nodded back. To swim in cool water would refresh her in many ways and perhaps rid her of the headache.

The young women led her along the path, which came out at a small beach by a pool where some other women and children were bathing and also washing their clothing. When they saw Delia they crowded round her to admire her clothing and jewellery as usual and then gestured to her to remove her clothing and be as they were, completely bare. A little self-consciously in front of all those curious eyes she stripped off her shirt and stepped out of her pants, thankful that she was wearing her bikini.

But the two strips of cloth which covered her breasts and hips seemed to amuse them very much. Some of them came up to touch the black elasticated material and were fascinated by the straps which snapped back on to her shoulders when they pulled them. Several of them indicated to her by gestures that she should take the bikini off and let them try it on, but she shook her head smilingly, hoping they would understand, and stepped towards the river.

The pool wasn't as big as the one at Posto Orlando, but the water was clear and brown, moving all the time, so she knew it was safe for swimming. And in the water was the best place to be at that time of the day, thought Delia, as she dived and swam, floated and splashed. Above her the sky was molten blue. On the banks the tree foliage was a thick tangle of green shimmering under waves of heat, but the water was soft and cool and for a while she forgot her problems as she played happily with the brown-skinned, shouting children and smiling graceful women.

Coming out of the water, she sat with the group and showed them how to build sand castles and tried by drawing on the flat sand with a twig to show them the world from which she came, feeling quite pleased with her pictures of planes, cars and houses even though her companions seemed to think they were funny and hooted with laughter.

But the heat and glare of the afternoon soon made her conscious of the headache which had bothered her since morning and she returned to the water to swim again, followed by a troup of thin boisterous boys.

It was while she was swimming that she heard some shouting coming from the shore, and glancing across, she noticed that some of the men of the tribe had come down to the beach and that there was an argument going on between them and the women. Deciding it was no business of hers, Delia dived under the surface and struck out for the far bank of the pool. She would touch it and then swim back. After that she had better start to find her way back to the clearing.

Swimming along, she found she was being accompanied by some of the boys and that they were laughing and shouting and pointing at her and then at the water. Stopping in mid-stroke, she trod water and looked around. Ahead of her there was a ring of ripples and under them a vague wavering shape. It looked as if there was a big fish just under the surface.

By now the boys were beside themselves with laughter, throwing themselves backwards into the water and sinking spectacularly. As she stared in bewilderment the water erupted near her and Edmund appeared, shaking his head and snorting to clear his eyes and nose of water, his bare chest heaving as he gulped in breaths of the steamy air.

'What are you doing here?' Delia exclaimed.

'Looking for you,' he retorted, treading water beside her.

'You must be crazy, going off like that without telling any of us where you'd gone. I've been looking everywhere for you. Why did you leave the village?'

'I . . . I . . . couldn't stand listening to Zanetta any longer,' she muttered. 'Edmund, I'll go back to Posto Orlando in the plane and she can stay with you, if that's what you want.'

He stared at her, frowning in puzzlement.

'What the hell are you on about now?' he exclaimed. 'The plane has gone, left about an hour ago. Carlo daren't risk waiting any longer while we searched for you. It's a long flight to the post from here and he'll only just make it before twilight.' His eyes narrowed and he gave her a curious glance. 'What did Zanetta say to you?'

'She said she should be staying here with you instead of me, that's all. I told her she could. Has she?'

'No, of course not. She knew better than to argue,' he said grimly. 'I'd told her what she had to do and, unlike you, she knows how to obey orders. She's gone, and for the past hour I've been thinking you'd gone too, were lost somewhere in that jungle.' He broke off and glared at her with something like hate in his eyes. 'Don't ever do that to me again, do you hear?' he said in a low fierce voice.

'Oh, I suppose it was all right for you to disappear for weeks, months, over a year without letting me know where you were, but I have only to walk out of sight for a short while for you to get all worked up,' she retorted, and promptly sank beneath the surface because in her attempt to defend herself she had forgotten to tread water. She came up spluttering to find him still beside her, but the expression in his eyes had changed. He was looking at her with a sort of tender mockery.

'You do choose the most awkward places to have an argument,' he jeered.

'I didn't choose it, you did. You swam out here after me,' she countered. 'And I wasn't arguing, only stating my point of view. Now you know how I felt when I didn't know where you were, how anxious and worried I was, not for an hour but for nearly sixteen months.'

'Peter knew where I was. You had only to ask him,' he said quietly, and spread his arms out sideways so that he could float on his back.

'I did, several times. He said you'd asked him not to tell me where you'd gone, and later he said that my guess as to where you were was as good as his,' she said flatly, and rolling over in the water she began to swim for the shore.

Edmund caught up with her and they swam side by side, touching the bottom at the same time and wading towards the beach together.

The women, who were all dressed now either in cotton shifts or sarongs made from cloth, home-spun from wild cotton, came down to the edge of the water to meet her. Chattering and gesturing, they took her hands and led her away from Edmund into the trees. There one of them offered her a strip of the woven cotton and by various gestures indicated that she should take it and wear it. Touched by this gesture of friendship, Delia nodded and while the women stood round her in a circle she wound the cloth round her body sarong-style, leaving her shoulders bare.

The women all clapped their hands and laughed. One of them took the scarlet banana flower she was wearing in her hair and tucked it behind Delia's ear. Again they all clapped and laughed, pointing to the flowers they were wearing and to their sarongs as if to suggest that at last she was like them. Then the leader took her by the hand and led her back to Edmund, who had just pulled on his shirt and pants.

The woman took one of his hands and pressed Delia's into it as if to link them together, and suddenly everyone, even the children, were silent. Slowly Edmund drew Delia towards him.

'I've a feeling they're expecting me to show some approval of the way they've dressed you,' he drawled. 'I feel quite out of it in my old jeans and shirt.'

'Perhaps you should be wearing an armband, black and red paint and a few feathers in your hair,' she teased softly.

'Would you like me any better if I did?' he challenged, much to her surprise.

'No,' she whispered, feeling her heart beating loudly in her ears. 'I like you as you are and I always have.'

He bent his head and kissed her lightly on the lips, and after that the rest of the day took on an enchanted, dreamlike quality for Delia. Escorted by the excited, chattering women and children, she walked with Edmund through the green, sun-shafted gloom of the forest back to the village where they were taken on a conducted tour of the huts by one of the headmen who could speak a little Portuguese and in whose care the chief had left them.

He explained that his tribe was known as the Pot-makers and took them to the hut of the most experienced potter, an elderly man who sat on the floor in the middle of his hut working a piece of clay between his hands. All around him, gleaming like jewels in the darkness of the hut, were specimens of his art—huge shallow bowls for serving manioc and maize, smaller bowls shaped like animals such as armadilloes and turtles and several bulbous urns. Many of them were painted black on the outside and striped with shining red paint on the inside. The care and skill with which they had been made fascinated Delia.

'Don't admire too many of them,' Edmund whispered to

her, 'or you'll find yourself having to take them all home with you and you'll have a devil of a time explaining to the Customs.'

In spite of his warning they were both carrying gifts of pottery when they left the hut and stepped out into the clearing in time to see the last of a brilliant scarlet, orange and gold sunset.

They ate their evening meal in the hut of the headman, succulent pieces of fish smoked over wood-fires and bowls of wild rice and beans, and all followed by more delicious thirst-quenching passion-fruit.

When it was over they went outside to watch the dancing as the yellow moon, slightly lopsided because it had begun to wane, peeped above the dark rim of the trees.

Six men dressed in skirts of yellow grass, wearing tall headdresses made of red and yellow feathers, and wings made from fresh, bright green leaves, leapt and stamped in the middle of the clearing to music with a strong throbbing beat which was played on lengths of hollow wood to the accompaniment of drums. A little boy joined in the dancing, catching at the men's swirling skirts and making the audience laugh until his mother ran into the middle of the clearing and caught him up in her arms.

The beat of the drums, the stamping of the dancers' feet, the shimmer of the moonlight on the feathered headdresses and on bare skin stirred the senses. Sitting beside Edmund on a log, Delia became suddenly aware of his closeness, of the brushing of his bare forearm against her arm when he moved, of the pressure of his thigh against hers. When she felt his arm go around her back and his fingers touch her waist lightly she wasn't surprised, but her heart began to beat in time to the deep seductive throbbing of the drums.

His fingers pressed suggestively against her waist and she

relaxed, allowing him to pull her against him. His breath
tickled her ear tantalisingly as he whispered,

'Let's go to bed.'

'Where?' she asked, turning her head to look at him, and
her cheek came in contact with his bristly jaw.

'In the hut they've offered us.'

'Do you know where it is?'

'Yes, over there, behind the chief's hut.'

'Hadn't we better tell someone we're going? They might
be offended if we leave before the dance is over.'

'I don't think so. I told the headman we might slip away
before the end.' He chuckled softly and again she felt a
delicious shivery feeling as his breath tickled her ear. 'He
was very understanding. Come on.'

Taking her hand, he led her through the long grasses into
the purple shadows between two huts and out again into the
golden radiance of the honey-coloured moon. The air was
warm and heavy with the scents of the jungle and Delia felt
a sensual excitement throbbing through her body in time to
the beat of the drums and the high-pitched whistling of the
pipes.

Inside the small beehive-shaped hut black shadows danced
upon the curving walls cast there by the flickering flame of
the usual kerosene lamp which was attached to the central
roof-supporting post.

'Oh, there's only one hammock,' exclaimed Delia, coming
to a dead stop and staring at the wide woven bed with its
veil of white mosquito netting. 'We'd better go and tell the
headman we need another one.'

'But we don't,' replied Edmund coolly as he pulled his
shirt off. 'This one is big enough for the two of us.'

While she stood there half fearful and half hopeful, ab-
sorbing the implication which lay behind the suggestion that

they should share the hammock, he unbelted his jeans, stepped out of them, rolled them up with his shirt, buckled his belt round the lot and hung the bundle from the strings of the hammock. The clothing she had taken off when she had gone swimming was already hanging there, she noticed with a jolt of surprise.

Edmund stepped towards her, the bare skin of his shoulders gleaming golden in the lamplight. His eyes glinted deeply blue and his mouth curved in a tantalising smile.

'Are you going to bed in that sarong thing or shall I help you to take it off?' he asked softly.

Her hands went to her breast to pull out the corner of the material which was tucked in there.

'Are you sure?' she whispered, staring up at him.

'Am I sure of what?' he answered.

'Are you sure you want me to sleep with you in the same hammock?' she asked shakily, unwinding the strip of cloth from her body. 'The other night when we went camping you didn't seem to want . . .'

'Forget the other night,' he ordered brusquely, taking the strip of cloth from her and going across the hammock to hang it over the strings. 'The biggest difficulty as usual will be getting into and under the netting without these damned pests joining us.'

He slapped a hand against the side of his neck and then against his thigh to kill two mosquitoes which were biting him and turned to her again. 'Are you ready to get in?'

He held out his hand to her. Hesitantly Delia placed her hand in his and went with him to the hammock. His calm matter-of-fact attitude in such a romantic setting with the sound of jungle music throbbing in the background bewildered her, but suddenly she seemed to have no will of her own. Completely submissive, she obeyed his instructions and managed to get into the hammock and under the netting, finding that there were two soft blankets made from wild cotton there, one to lie on and one for a covering.

'Take your boots off and hand them to me.' Edmund ordered, and again she obeyed automatically.

After handing him the boots she lay back. It seemed to her that the noise of her quickly beating heart filled the whole hut and she felt a return of the sickly headache which had bothered her earlier in the day.

It was true the hammock was wider than others she had slept in, wide enough for two people to lie close together in each other's arms. The thought of lying in Edmund's arms made the beat of her heart increase wildly and she felt desire flare through her suddenly from a hard core somewhere near the lower part of her stomach.

The kerosene lamp went out and the acrid smell of its smoke tingled her nose and made her sneeze. Edmund laughed as he sat on the edge of the hammock and lifted the mosquito netting.

'Now for it,' he whispered. 'Let's hope the whole thing doesn't collapse under our weight!'

The strings of the hammock creaked a little as they slipped slightly on the poles to which it was attached and it swayed as Edmund shuffled in beside her. Delia felt the warmth of his legs and bare feet against hers. He pushed an arm under her shoulder and then she was lying against him with her head on his chest just above his heart, which she could hear pounding away steadily and not at all wildly as hers was.

It began slowly and delicately, as they lay close together in their cotton cocoon, with a few whispered words.

'Are you comfortable?' he asked, and she felt the movement of his jaw against her head.

'Yes, thank you,' she said, and felt the rumble of his laugh in his chest under her ear.

'Yes, thank you,' he mocked the way she spoke. 'You're always so polite with your thank yous and pleases.'

'I can't help it,' she mumbled. 'To be polite was drilled into me at school. And by Aunt Marsha.'

'Have you seen her lately?'

'No. She wrote me off as a bad loss when I took no notice of her warnings about you.'

'She warned you against me? When?' he exclaimed, obviously surprised.

'The evening of the day we met at Southleigh. She said I shouldn't get involved with you and when I refused to do as she said she told me I was a fool.'

There was a short silence, then he said in a low voice,

'Perhaps she was right. You'd be better off married to someone like Peter. He'd cosset you, stay with you, make a home for you—and I still can't understand why you didn't go through with a divorce.'

'I couldn't, not without seeing you first.'

'Pete said that wouldn't be necessary once I'd told him as my lawyer that I agreed to be divorced. He said he'd let me know how things turned out, but I never heard from him, not once.'

'Did you write to him?' she asked.

'A couple of times, but you know me—I'm not the world's best correspondent.'

'Why didn't you write to me?'

Again there was a short silence, then she felt his fingers in a tress of her hair, twining it round and round.

'I didn't think you'd want to hear from me after what happened,' he murmured. 'God, if you knew how badly I felt!' The words sounded as if they were wrenched out of him and the desire to comfort him was strong within her. Raising a hand, she touched his cheek with her fingers, stroking it gently at first, then laying her palm against it.

'It was my fault,' she whispered, and felt an immediate lightening of her spirits as she admitted at last to him that she had made a mistake. 'I shouldn't have behaved as I did. I was frightened and I didn't understand you. We knew so little about each other and Peter had just said that you probably weren't faithful to me while you were away ...'

'Peter, Peter, Peter!' he interrupted her fiercely. 'It all seems to revolve about him and what he said to me and what he said to you. We were communicating through him instead of directly with each other.'

'I know. He'd come between us. I tried to communicate with you. I went back that night when I'd calmed down to tell you I was sorry, but you weren't there. I waited up all night for you, but you didn't come. I hoped you'd be there the next day when I came home from work, but ... but ... you'd gone. Oh, Edmund, it was awful!'

Tears spurted from her eyes, ran down her face on to the bare skin of his chest. His arms tightened about her and he murmured soft words of comfort. He stroked her hair tenderly, tilted her chin with his fingers and licked the teardrops from her eyes. He kissed her quivering mouth gently, his lips warm and soft. Her lips pursed beneath his, returning the kiss, and she slid her hand round his neck, pressing it against the nape to show she didn't want him to move away. She could feel the hard thrust of his hips against hers and the tingling touch of his fingers against her breast as they slid under the edge of her bikini bodice.

They were close in the warmth and darkness of their airborne bed and there was only one way in which they could be closer. Edmund stopped kissing to speak, his voice a soft seductive sound, his breath warm and smelling of tobacco smoke as it drifted across her face.

'Delia, you know what I want, but is it what you want?' he said. 'I wouldn't like to frighten you again.'

She pressed against him, feeling a sensuous delight in the touching of their warm bodies.

'Oh yes, please, Edmund, make love to me now. I've wanted you so much for so long. That's why I came to Brazil when I found out where you were. I wanted to be with you.'

He didn't hesitate any longer. His lips found hers again and drew from her an immediate passionate response. The hammock swayed a little and its strings creaked. Through the opening in the roof of the hut stray moonbeams slanted in as if to bless the simple natural reunion, and outside the rhythmic beating of jungle drums came to an abrupt stop.

CHAPTER SIX

DELIA awoke suddenly to pain and noise. The pain was in her stomach, agonising, sharp as razor blades, making her gasp and her knees jerk up. The noise was thunder crashing about overhead.

Trying to ignore both, she shifted slightly in the hammock, making it sway. Edmund was lying on her arm with his head against her breast, completely relaxed and sleeping heavily.

Delia smiled into the darkness. It was worth the pins and needles in her arm to have him there, and their physical reunion had been so triumphantly successful in spite of the narrow confines of the hammock that she couldn't help wondering why it hadn't happened that first night in Posto Orlando.

It takes time to forget and forgive. And she supposed he was right and they both had to forget and forgive the fact that instead of trusting each other they had trusted Peter, the so-called best friend who had been jealous of both of them.

A flash of lightning streaked across the sky outside and, through the smoke hole in the roof, temporarily lit the inside of the hut with harsh blue light. Thunder clattered, sounding like hundreds of metal barrels being beaten by steel rods. Pain knifed through Delia's stomach and sickness rose within her.

'I'll have to get up,' she whispered, but Edmund was too fast asleep to hear. She managed to slide her arm from beneath him and then herself and swung out of the hammock.

There wasn't time to get the bundle of the clothing or to put on her boots. Barefoot, she ran out of the hut. Lightning flashed again and she saw the shapes of trees, the bare red brown earth around the hut lit up by the blue light. Into the forest she ran to huddle by a tree to be sick, wishing suddenly she was back in the comparative civilised comfort of Posto Orlando where there were separate lavatories in the huts and wash-hand basins.

By the time the nausea was over she was shaking. Standing up, she reeled and caught hold of a swinging branch of creeper to steady herself. Her head was aching so much that it felt uncontrollable and she could hardly see. She stepped forward to make her way back to the hut and another crippling attack of sickness seized her.

Several times she tried to go back to the hut, only to be sick again, and all around her the thunder boomed and the lightning flashed. Weak and dizzy, she at last managed to creep back to the hut through the rain which had begun to fall like hundreds of hard grey sticks. Streaming with water, she made her way to the hammock.

'Where have you been?' Edmund slid out of the hammock to stand beside her as she clung to it for support.

'I . . . I . . . think I have dysentery,' she mumbled. 'I've been terribly sick and . . . and . . .' She broke off to moan and press her hands against her stomach.

He said nothing but acted quickly, taking one of the thin blankets from the bed and wrapping her into it. He lifted her into the hammock, then eased in beside her and gathered her against him.

'You've been feeling queasy all day, haven't you?' he said crisply.

'Yes. I woke with a headache and a feeling of sickness.'

'Then why the hell did you come on this trip?' he asked harshly.

'I wanted to ... to be with you ... to go where you were going...' she stuttered, her teeth chattering as a chill swept over her. 'For the first time you asked me if I'd like to go with you and I wasn't going to refuse just because I had a niggling headache.'

'You shouldn't have come,' he groaned. 'I should never have let you come. I asked you because I knew that if I didn't Carlo would. I tried to put you off by seeming not too overjoyed by the idea. I had a feeling something like this would happen.'

'But if I hadn't come we wouldn't have ...' she began, when pain knifed through her stomach again, her knees jerked up and she gasped.

His arms tightened about her and he let out an oath as if the pain had been his.

'I should have sent you back with Carlo instead of Zanetta,' he grated.

'She's in love with you,' she muttered. Now she was becoming very warm and her head was whirling.

'How do you know she is?' he asked curiously.

'She told me, and I saw the way she greeted you when you arrived at Binauros.'

'That was the *abraço*, nothing else. Brazilians embrace everyone they know.'

'And she told me you walked with her under the stars at Ipanema,' she moaned, and her voice seemed to be coming from far away. Now she was so hot she felt she was in a sauna bath getting hotter and hotter and hotter. 'And I watched her talking to you at suppertime yesterday. She had no time for anyone else, and you listened to her and talked back.'

'I was being polite. I didn't hear much of what she said,' he retorted with a laugh. 'I was too busy watching you. Anyone would have thought you and Carlo were long-lost friends who had just found each other again. He hogged all your attention that night—he even had the nerve to kiss your hand after escorting you to the sleeping hut.'

'How do you know he did? You weren't there,' she challenged weakly. She was feeling that she might burst into flames any minute and her mind kept blanking out.

'Yes, I was right behind you.'

'I thought you'd gone somewhere with Zanetta,' she mumbled.

'No. I talked to Carlo for a while after you'd gone into the hut.'

'He's very kind.'

'And I'm not?' he queried dryly.

'Not to me. You're kind to everyone else, but not to me,' she mumbled, twisting her head about. 'Is Zanetta the reason why you don't want to go back to England? If she is I'll do it if it's what you really want. Is it? Is it?'

The palm of his hand came against her forehead. It was blessedly cool.

'I'm so hot, Edmund, and thirsty. Please get me something to drink and tell me if it's what you want me to do,' she mumbled.

'You're not making sense, darling,' he murmured. 'You're feverish and don't know what you're saying.'

'Yes, I do.' It was suddenly very important to get this particular message over to him. Now that Peter was no longer between them they could communicate directly with each other. 'I have to know, have to know before I go back. Tell me, please tell me!'

'Tell you what?' he asked gently.

'Tell me if you want me to go ahead with arrangements for a divorce so that you can marry Zanetta. Oh, Edmund, where are you going?'

'To get something to give you for that pain and also to bring down your temperature. I won't be long.'

Delia lay back in the hammock. It seemed to be whirling round and round in the air. Everything was black before her eyes and the thunder was inside her head, banging and clattering about. She felt cool fingers on her arm and raised her head, trying to see who was touching her. Her head fell back out of control and she lost consciousness.

When she came round she was being carried from the hut, out of darkness into blinding brilliance of sunlight. Realising she was on a stretcher, she stared hazily up at the hot blue sky, seeing the curving fringed leaves of tall banana palms wheeling by. The movement stopped and the stretcher was laid on the ground. A face floated into view above her. It was pale walnut brown with sparkling black eyes and a white smile under a drooping moustache. Carlo.

'*Bom dia*, Delia. Too bad you are sick, but I'm glad you are awake. Do you think you can climb up into the plane with my help?' he said.

'Where's Edmund?' she asked weakly. She wasn't as hot as she had been. In fact she was soaked with sweat and she was still wrapped in the cotton blanket. Just as well, she thought with a weary flicker of humour, because she hadn't a stitch of clothing on her otherwise.

'I'm here.' Edmund's voice was deep and soft and his fingers were hard and lean as they closed round hers. His face floated into view, long-jawed and lean, tanned to a golden brown and blurred with a stubble of brown beard. But his eyes were tired with shadows under them, very tired. *He tires easily. He needs a rest.* Luiz had said that to her, and it was true.

'Edmund, you should rest,' she whispered. 'You're tired.'

'I will when I've done what I have to do,' he replied.

'Right now we're going to fly to Posto Orlando and get you into a proper bed so you can sleep yourself well. Let me help you to sit up.'

Moving was an effort and her head wasn't very clear, but he put his arm about her shoulders and heaved her into a sitting position.

'I feel awful,' she said with a little laugh. 'Everything keeps coming and going.'

'That's because you're doped,' he explained. 'I gave you an injection last night because you were in a lot of pain. You'll be fine when you've slept it off. Now I'm going to lift you up and pass you to Carlo who's in the plane and he'll put you in the back seat.'

He lifted her and the transfer to Carlo's arms was made far more easily than she expected. Soon she was settled in the seat, the safety belt was fastened around her and Edmund sat down beside her.

The plane took off and for a brief hazy moment she saw the villagers waving farewell. She would have liked to have said good-bye properly to them, especially to the women who had been so kind to her the previous day, but she was too dopey to even raise a hand. Then the clearing had gone and there was only the limitless green jungle spread below. It wavered before her eyes, her eyelids drooped and once again she slid into unconsciousness.

She didn't really come round until a few hours later. Opening her eyes, she found she was on the truckle bed in the small dark room which she had shared with Edmund at Posto Orlando. She knew it was night because the light was on. She felt clean and neat and lifting the edge of the sheet which covered her she saw that she was wearing a clean cotton nightdress from the bag which she had left behind when she had gone to Binauros.

The sound of paper rustling made her look round. At the small table Edmund was sitting. He was writing in an exercise book and he was frowning as he concentrated. Tobacco smoke coiled in the air from the cigarette in his mouth and hung in layers in the heavy still air of the room.

'What are you doing?' Delia asked, her voice a thin thread of sound, and he turned to look at her.

'Hello,' he said, smiling slightly. 'So you've come back. I'm writing up some of my report. How do you feel?' He left the chair and came to sit on the edge of the bed and look down at her critically. He didn't look as tired as he had when she had last been conscious of seeing him.

'I feel very thin, as if I have no insides, like after I lost the baby,' she replied slowly, still not quite in control of her tongue or her thoughts.

'What baby?' His voice was sharp, making her lift her eyelids which had begun to droop again. He was leaning forward, his eyes dark and incredulous. His face seemed to have gone very pale. Delia realised what she had said and wished for a moment she could unsay it. But it was done now and there was no chance of retreating from the subject because his hands were on her shoulders and he was saying in a hoarse yet commanding voice, 'Delia, you've got to tell me. What baby?'

'Ours,' she whispered, her eyes wide as she saw the shock go through him. Raising her hand, she touched his face urgently. 'Oh, Edmund, I'm sorry I lost it. It was premature and it lived only a few minutes . . .'

'Why didn't you tell me?' he interrupted her harshly, and his eyes were a hard burning blue as he glared at her. 'I should have been told. I had a right to know.'

'I . . . I . . . tried,' she said, saw an expression of scepticism twist across his face and cried out, 'I did, God knows I did!

I wanted to tell you. Oh, please believe me—I couldn't find you. No one knew where you'd gone. The Red Cross didn't know. The institute where you'd done that research didn't know. They could only give me an address in Hampshire, so I wrote there. Oh, I tried, Edmund. I did really . . .'

'Peter knew where I was,' he said grimly.

'I know, but I've told you already he wouldn't tell me where you were. He said he couldn't betray your confidence, that I had to communicate with you through him, and after I'd found out that he wanted me to divorce you so he could marry me I didn't trust him any more. I stopped seeing him and I didn't tell him I was going to have a baby. Did you tell him he wasn't to tell me where you were?'

Edmund shook his head slowly from side to side. His face was drawn as if he were in great pain. His hands left her shoulders, he raked one through his hair and stood up to walk away from the bed to stand with his back to her, shoulders slumped.

'No, I didn't tell him that,' he muttered. 'All I ever said to him was that if you wanted a divorce I would agree to it and that he was to let me know if there was any change.' He swung round suddenly and again he glared at her accusingly. 'If I'd known, if someone had told me about the child I'd have come back to be with you, to look after you so that it would have lived. That's what you meant the other day when I asked you if you'd been ill recently and you said "in a way", isn't it?'

She nodded, too weak and too scared to speak. She had never expected he would react to the knowledge of the child in this way. He drew a long shuddering breath and glared at her, and once more he looked as if he hated her.

'And then you had the nerve to say it was none of my business,' he said harshly. 'You dared to say that, knowing the child was mine, was part of me. Why didn't you tell me about it when I asked you?'

'I . . . I couldn't. You'd been so hostile the day before and I didn't want you to think I was using the fact that I'd had your child to . . . to get you back,' she whispered the last words and added forlornly, 'I didn't realise you'd care so much.'

'Not care? What the hell do you think I'm made of? Stone?' he demanded hoarsely. 'I'm a human being. I have feelings which can be hurt just like yours. You left me out of something important to both of us. You didn't trust me enough to tell me.' His mouth twisted in a bitter grimace. 'But maybe it wasn't important to you. Maybe you wanted to lose it . . .'

He turned away, opened the door and went out into the frog-croaking, cricket-chirping darkness. The door slammed behind him. For a few moments Delia lay blinking at the electric light, feeling the tears slide down her cheeks. Then with a little moan she turned on her side and the blessed darkness of sleep once again blanketed her mind.

When she woke again she knew it was morning because pale saffron sunlight was shafting through the slates of the heavy shutters and she could hear the parakeets squabbling as they perched on the roof of the hut. From the washroom came the sound of water gurgling away down the outlet of the wash basin, followed by the sound of someone whistling.

She looked across at the other bed. It was unmade and had obviously been slept in. On the end of it was Edmund's travelling bag, unzipped with clothes tumbling out of it, creased shirts, ragged shorts and creased cotton trousers, the high fashion of the jungle.

Delia smiled slightly at the thought and felt a sudden longing to take the clothes to the river and wash them as she had seen the women washing clothes at the village she had visited two days previously. Pushing back the sheet, she swung her legs out of bed and stood up. She felt weak but not dizzy any more and her temperature was definitely down.

She stepped over to the other bed and sat down on it, pulling the bag towards her. She began to take clothes out of the bag and examine them. They were really in a terrible state, she thought, torn and dirty, and some of them should be thrown away.

'Seems I can't turn my back on you for a minute without you doing something you shouldn't be doing,' Edmund's voice rasped angrily as he came out of the washroom and saw her, and she gave him a wary glance as she remembered how angry he had been the night before. 'Get back into bed at once,' he ordered curtly. 'You're not fit to be moving about yet.'

'Yes, I am,' she retorted, tilting her chin at him. 'Your clothes are in an awful mess.'

'So what?' he challenged, standing over her with his hands on his hips. He was wearing only jeans which were very faded and so shrunken that they stretched tightly over his lean hips and across his flat stomach. Above the belt at his waist his skin was ringed by insect bites and the hair on his chest was still damp from his wash. Under the tanned taut skin his pectoral muscles made ridges and his collar-bones gleamed whitely. Higher up the curve of his mouth mocked her and his eyes were cold, like chips of blue ice.

One hand left his hip, reached down and twitched the shirt she was holding from her hands. He tossed it towards the open bag.

'Leave them alone,' he ordered brusquely. 'You don't have to do anything about them.'

'But as your wife I should look after your clothes and see that they're neat and clean,' she objected miserably.

'As my wife you should have made me welcome when I came home sixteen months ago,' he said in that soft stinging way he had, 'and told me about our child. Now will you get back into bed, *Mrs* Talbot.' His face was hard and unforgiving.

'Oh, I wish I hadn't told you,' she cried. 'I didn't mean to hurt you,' she added. 'I'm sorry.'

'I seem to remember making a similar appeal to you once,' he jeered. 'Now get into bed.'

'All right.' She stood up and went over to the other bed. 'But that shirt hasn't any buttons on it.'

'Hardly surprising, since you pulled them off the other night,' he replied dryly.

Lying down and pulling the sheet over her, she watched him take the least creased and least dirty shirt from the bag.

'Do you know what was wrong with my insides and why I was sick?' she asked.

'It was either food poisoning combined with dysentery or you ate something which disagreed with you, maybe the wild boar meat we had at Binauros. It was pretty fatty,' he said coolly as he pulled on the shirt. 'Do you feel hungry?'

'Not yet.'

More memories were awakening now, of the night they had spent together in the same hammock. Had it meant nothing after all? Had it been a purely physical act involving nothing of the emotions as far as he was concerned, forgotten almost as soon as it was over? Watching him rolling up his clothing and stuffing it into the bag, she wished he would come and sit on the bed beside her, smile at her, take her hand in his and kiss her.

He seemed to be packing everything he owned, including

the book in which he had been writing last night, and when the bag was zipped up he locked it. Then he turned and came to sit beside her on the bed.

He did take her hand in his, but it was only to feel her pulse. He didn't smile at her but watched the second hand on his wrist watch. When the minute was up he felt her brow impersonally before getting to his feet again. Disappointment because he hadn't lingered beside her washed through her, making her feel weepy again.

'You seem all right now, but you're bound to feel weak until you've had something to eat,' he said in his cool crisp doctor's voice. 'Go easy on the food at first. Not too much of the rice and beans. The manioc gruel should be all right, though. Anyway, it won't be for long. You're flying to Rio tomorrow, back to civilisation and all mod. cons.'

'Won't you be going with me?' she asked, sitting up as she felt a chill of fear go through her.

'No,' he said curtly, and turning away lifted his travelling bag with one hand and his doctor's bag with the other. 'I'm going to Fenenal with Manoel. Carlo is flying us there. We set off in about five minutes.'

'But why are you going back there?' she cried.

'Word was brought to Luiz yesterday when he was still at Binauros that there's been an outbreak of influenza among the tribes on Fenenal. Not being used to that type of disease, they're dying of it,' Edmund replied grimly. 'When Luiz flew back here from Binauros with Manoel and Rita he asked me to go and do what I can for the tribes.'

'Let me come with you,' she said urgently, slipping out of the bed and padding over to him on bare feet. 'Please, Edmund,' she pleaded, putting a hand on his chest and pleating the cotton of the shirt between her fingers. 'Let me come.'

'No.' His voice was hard and cold. 'You're going on the Air Force plane which comes tomorrow with supplies. It's all arranged. Rita is going too. She wants to see her children and she's invited you to stay with her so you can recover from your sickness. You need a rest and some good food to build you up.'

'But you need a rest too,' she argued. 'Aren't there any other doctors? What about Dr Mireilles? Couldn't she go?'

'She is going. She's here now and they're all waiting for me,' he said coolly. 'You'll be better off with Rita by the sea in Rio.'

'But I want to be with you, not her,' she insisted. The knowledge that Zanetta was going, would be with him when she couldn't be with him, was awakening that awful distorting jealousy.

'Well, I don't want you with me,' he replied harshly, pushing her away. 'Now go back to bed.'

Delia staggered slightly, catching her breath as pain sliced though her in reaction to his cruel retort. At once he dropped his bag and stepped towards her, taking hold of her arms.

'I've said it all wrong again, haven't I?' he groaned. 'Listen. I have to go, you know that. I'm a doctor and I have to try and heal people, any people, anywhere. It would be the same if we lived in England. I would have to go when I was called. I have to leave you.'

'But it's different here,' she argued. 'I could come with you. Oh, if you really loved me you'd let me come with you. But you don't love me. You never have.'

'There isn't time to discuss that now,' he replied, letting go of her. 'I can't risk taking you. You're not better yet and you could pick up anything in your weakened state, and I'm not going to have that on my conscience. As for your accusation about me not loving you, I can retort in kind. If you loved me you'd let me go without making such a damned fuss.' He gave a mirthless crack of laughter. 'We seem to have gone through all this before, don't we? It's the same argument which landed us into marriage.'

He picked up his bags again and made for the door. Delia followed him.

'When will I see you again?' she asked.

'I don't know. Maybe next week. I'll go to Rio as soon as I've done what I can.'

'I . . . I'm supposed to fly back to London next Wednesday,' she muttered. 'I have a job to do, too, you know.'

'I'll try to be in Rio before you go,' he said tautly, not looking at her. 'But I'm not promising anything. Nothing is straightforward in this country and time is of no account.' He opened the door and gave her a long level look. 'You know, if you really love me, Delia, you'll wait for me in Rio,' he added.

Ten minutes later, as she lay dry-eyed and sunk in the depths of misery on the truckle bed, Delia heard the humming sound of Carlo's plane when it flew over the clearing. Soon afterwards there was the sound of footsteps on the verandah of the hut. Knuckles rapped on the door and it opened slowly. Rita appeared and closed the door behind her and came to the bedside. She seemed lovely as usual and elegant even in her 'jungle' wear of cotton pants and cotton shirt, but her big brown eyes were full of tears.

'Ah, how pale you are, and sad-looking,' she murmured as she sat on the side of the bed. 'But you do not cry.' Even as she spoke great tears welled in her eyes, slid over the edge of her lids and down her smooth golden cheeks. 'Always I cry considerably when Manoel goes away. Manoel does too. But you do not cry and Edmund looks so cold and self-contained.

Yet it is best not to speak to him, for he snarls at anyone who does. Will you snarl at me too? Is that how you show you are dying a little inside because you have said goodbye to someone you love very much?'

Delia shook her head, tried to smile and couldn't.

'I asked him to take me with him and he wouldn't,' she said in a small, miserable little voice. 'He said he didn't want me with him and I know why. It's because Zanetta has gone too.'

'But this is nonsense you are talking,' said Rita, her tears suddenly forgotten. She put out a hand and pushed Delia's hair back from her head and frowned a little. 'Strange. You have no fever, so why do you talk nonsense?'

'It isn't nonsense, Edmund doesn't love me and . . .'

'You say that after he worried so much when you were ill, blaming himself for letting you go to that village? Oh, can't you see he wouldn't let you go with him today because he cares too much about you? He doesn't want you to be ill.'

'He'd be like that about anyone who had been ill or who is ill,' insisted Delia. 'He doesn't love me and he never has. He was in love with me for a while because he thought I was pretty and we had fun together. But he doesn't love me. He loves his work more.'

Rita gave her a sidelong assessing glance, then said with a knowing sort of nod,

'I understand what you mean. Manoel is the same. But what man isn't? Especially men who have a calling or a profession. And they assume we understand. "*We'll be back*," they say. "*When?*" we ask. "Oh, this week, next week, some time," they say. "What shall we do?" we say. "Wait," they reply.' Rita laughed. 'Isn't that the way it goes?' she asked, smiling down at Delia.

'Yes, but . . .' began Delia, and found Rita's forefinger pressed against her lips.

'Not another word until you are fed and are feeling stronger. You're depressed because he has left you while you are weak and not thinking sensibly. After some gruel and more sleep you'll feel much better, and tomorrow you and I will fly away too, to Rio where we shall enjoy ourselves while we're waiting.' She stood up and having a second thought she slanted a glance down at Delia again. 'You should not worry about Zanetta,' she said quietly. 'She has nothing that Edmund needs. You have. And now I will go to fetch you some food.'

Although cheered by Rita's remarks, Delia was still worried because Edmund had gone away from her while he was in an unforgiving frame of mind after hearing about the loss of their child. She couldn't help remembering that he had left her once before after a quarrel and she had worried continually in case he would come back to her. He had come back and she hadn't been there. She had been out for the day with another man.

Groaning with regret, she writhed on the hot bed thinking how much Peter was to blame for her estrangement from Edmund. Yet they had been offered the second honeymoon made possible by Luis Santos and Ben Davies. Was she going to let jealousy of Zanetta ruin it? Was she going to let a third person come between herself and Edmund again?

No, she mustn't. She must learn from her past mistakes. She must put Zanetta out of her mind and trust Edmund. He had said he would see her again in Rio if she waited for him, and no matter how long it took him to come there she must be there waiting, in the same way that Rita would be waiting for Manoel. She must trust him and he would trust her.

Next morning Posto Orlando shrank to a series of dots beneath the silvery wing of the Air Force plane and soon the village was hidden from sight by the masses of green trees.

Delia blinked back tears. The parting from Luiz Santos had been a sad one. Members of the tribe which lived in the village had given her parting presents; a comb beautifully made from pine needles, a hand-woven headband, a dainty basket all hand-made and fashioned with care, they were worth so much more than the toffees, cigarettes and soap which she had given them.

It was over, her expedition to the jungle, and she wasn't sure whether it had been successful or not. It was true she had found Edmund again, but nothing had been resolved between them. She wasn't sure yet if he loved her. She would have to wait until she saw him again, and considering his frame of mind when he had left for Fenenal she couldn't be sure of that either.

At Brasilia she and Rita arrived in time to board a regular scheduled flight for Rio. Within a few hours they were being greeted by Rita's sister Maria Martinez, who had brought Rita's children with her.

The meeting between Rita and the three golden-skinned, black-haired, black-eyed boys was ecstatic. They all piled into the small car which Maria Martinez drove and were soon speeding along the wide road which linked the airport to the beautiful city of shimmering slim white towers set between high humpy green mountains and the turquoise ocean.

As they approached the city the traffic increased. Several lanes of small cars all seemed to compete with each other to get wherever they were going first. High buses with wheels revolving at the window level of the little car in which Delia was travelling squeezed between the lanes. Maria seemed to charge from red traffic light to red traffic light and changed lanes with an utter ruthlessness and disregard for other drivers which caused Delia to flinch.

'There is only one way to survive in the Rio traffic,' said Rita as she noticed Delia's consternation. 'You have to be aggressive. You are frightened?'

'Terrified,' gasped Delia.

'You should see it at rush hour,' said Rita, laughing. 'Isn't driving in London like this?'

'I would say we're a little more controlled,' said Delia, not wanting to appear too critical. 'Whatever is that conductor banging on the outside of the bus for?'

'They all do it. It means "get out of the way, we're coming. Don't say we didn't warn you." The bus drivers think they own the roads,' said Rita.

At last they left the arterial roadway and delved right into the city down a long *avenida* as straight as a beam of light between high buildings. The sidewalks were thronged with pedestrians, most of them shoppers. Soon they were on another wide highway which took them to the south side of the city and on to a narrow avenue which wound along the coast beside the sea.

On one side the ocean slid restlessly up and down stone slabs which formed the foundation of the road. On the other stretched a smooth emerald green golf course. The road turned a corner and there was another view of humpy green mountains and a curving yellow beach on to which glittering white surf pounded incessantly.

The avenue divided into two wide lanes flanked by straight-stemmed umbrellas of palm trees. On the inland side elegant houses were set among tailored green lawns behind low white walls.

Maria changed gear and turned the little car through an opening in the white wall and drove up a winding driveway to a long white house which had a red-tiled roof and curving Moorish arches over its windows and doors. She stopped the car beside a big white Cadillac.

'This is my parents' home where we will stay until the men come back from Fenenal,' said Rita to Delia. 'As you can see, it's big enough for several families.'

A little overawed by the beauty of the house and the obvious wealth of its owners, Delia followed Rita and the chattering little boys through one of the arches into a square patio with black and white stone mosaic floor where exotic flowers bloomed, their colours brilliant against the white walls.

From the patio they went through a door made from wire mesh into a cool hallway where the black and white mosaic floor was continued. Huge pottery jars crammed with greenery and flowers were set about the floor and black wrought iron screens set under more curving archways gave glimpses into expensively furnished rooms.

A dark-skinned woman was waiting in the hall. She was dressed in severe black and white, but her smile was warm and cheerful.

'This is Dulva, my mother's housekeeper,' Rita said, and after further conversation with the dark woman added, 'My mother is away with my father right now but will be back at the end of next week for the Carnival. You have heard of our Carnival, Delia? It goes on for four days and four nights before Ash Wednesday. It starts with a procession of dancers and musicians. There are parades, song competitions and masked balls. It's a pity that you'll miss it. But perhaps Edmund won't be back by Wednesday and you won't leave then. Perhaps he'll be back later and you'll see the Carnival together.'

After the humid heat of the jungle and of the outdoors in

Rio the air-conditioning of the house was refreshing. Leading Delia up a staircase with a wrought iron banister, Rita showed her into a pretty guest room with a double bed and dark antique Portuguese furniture and a view of the shimmering blue ocean through its window.

'Take your time to do what you wish,' Rita told her. 'There is a bathroom through that door. Bathe, wash your hair, rest on the bed. We shall dine early tonight because we haven't eaten much today. I shall come and tell you when the meal is ready.'

Soaking in scented warm water in the luxuriously appointed bathroom, Delia thought of Edmund sweating it out in the jungle and being bitten by mosquitoes. In comparison with living conditions in the jungle this beautiful house was like heaven.

After bathing she unpacked the clothes from the suitcase which she had left in Brasilia when she had flown to the jungle. It contained the dresses and skirts she had brought with her. She chose a Paisley patterned skirt in greens and blues. Gathered at the waist and with a flounce round the calf-length hem, it went well with the white cotton full-sleeved, scooped-neck gypsy-style blouse she was wearing.

But as she gazed at her reflection she wasn't pleased with her appearance. She was too pale and too thin. She complained about how she looked to Rita when they sat at a long table set with a beautiful hand-crocheted white cloth and gleaming antique silver cutlery to eat a dish of turkey and ham which Rita called *perú a brasiliera,* followed by a dessert of preserved tropical fruits served with a soft white cheese.

'A few days here and all that will soon be changed,' said Rita with her kind smile. 'We shall loll about in the sunshine, swim in the surf and loll about in the sun again. We shall eat well and perhaps do a little sightseeing and visiting. I shall take you up Corcovado to see the huge statue of Christ there. We shall ride on the cable car to the top of Sugar Loaf mountain. Oh, we shall do everything one should do on a visit to Rio and before we know it Manoel and Edmund will be here with us.'

And so for the next few days Delia combined the pleasant life of a wealthy surburbanite living on the outskirts of Rio with that of a tourist, and gradually she put on a little weight so that her body became softly curved again and her skin acquired a warm peach-coloured bloom. Rita was true to her word and took her to see all the sights, including some of the *favellas*, the numerous shacks clinging to the hillsides where the poor people lived.

'Manoel would not approve if you saw one side only of the way of life in our country,' Rita explained with a laugh, as they drove down a twisting lane where there was a magnificent view but where the sheds in which people lived clung by friction only to the rocks and where there was no water, no electricity and no plumbing.

With the passing of the week-end Delia began to grow a little tense again. Would Edmund come before Wednesday or even on Wednesday? In the night silence of her room she worried, and to take her mind off the worry she began to write her articles from the notes she had taken while she had been in the jungle. Monday and Tuesday passed. The temperature was climbing every day and with it the humidity. Only in the house or in the sea was there comfort.

Wednesday took its course. In the morning Delia and Rita went into Rio to shop in the pleasant Rua do Ouvidor where automobiles were not permitted. They had lunch in a huge restaurant on nearby Rua Goncalves Dias and then drove back to the house for *siesta*.

Trying to hide her tenseness, Delia went to the beach as usual after *siesta* and tried to forget her anxiety by playing in the surf with the three boys. When she returned to the house she entered hopefully, half expecting to be greeted by Edmund and Manoel. But no one had come and there had been no phone calls. The evening dragged by as she tried to be interested in some friends Rita and Maria had invited for dinner. One of the young men played the guitar and sang a song, and when she went to bed its refrain—*My days are spent in sadness and hope*—repeated itself over and over again in her mind. So her days were spent in sadness because Edmund was away and in hope that he might come back.

But Wednesday had come and gone and he wasn't back. She had waited. She had let the flight to England go and now she would have to cable Ben Davies and tell him why she hadn't returned. She would have to stay here and wait as Rita was waiting.

Next day seemed hotter and more humid than ever.

'We shall go up to Petropolis and visit Manoel's parents. It is in the mountains and you will find it cooler there and more to your liking,' announced Rita. 'And it will help to make the time pass for me as for you.'

'But supposing Edmund and Manoel come back while we aren't here? Edmund might think I've gone back to England,' said Delia anxiously. Once before she had gone out for the day and Edmund had returned to find her gone. Never would she forget the consequences.

'Dulva will tell them where we have gone and when we shall be back,' replied Rita serenely, and added with her bright smile, 'And for a change they can wait for us. It will do no harm.'

Delia pushed her misgivings to the back of her mind, determined to enjoy the outing to yet another part of this land-without-limit. The morning, though hot, was sunless as they drove along the Avenida Brasil out of Rio past a mixture of *favellas*, small industries and shops. The road passed over *biaxado* or lowlands where banana palms grew. They stopped to buy bananas from a stall and Rita introduced Delia for the first time to the tiny fruit she called *banana de ouro*.

After a while the green wall of some high mountains reared up through the mist, the Organ mountains. They passed through a tunnel and came out into sunshine on the other side of the mountains. Trim cottages lined the road, *casas de verao*, summer houses of superb design belonging to the wealthy.

Yet the home of Manoel's parents was simple. It seemed to grow out of the ground like an old English cottage. While the three boys floated in the swimming pool Delia and Rita sipped *caxaca*—lemon juice stiffened with sugar-cane alcohol. The garden was full of fruit trees, cool and shady.

They stayed the night and most of the next day, Manoel's mother pressing them to stay because she wanted news of Manoel and loved the company of her grandchildren. They left half-way through the afternoon, driving back the way they had come, dipping down into the city as lights were going on the high buildings, pricking the tall dark pinnacles with diamonds, while the rays of the setting sun, slanting from behind the humped back of a mountain gilded the frothy cumulus clouds which had built up over the sea after a day of great heat.

In the pleasantly cool house beside the sea Delia went up to her room. Another two days had gone by and still Edmund hadn't come. How long would she have to wait? Sighing, she slipped out of the dress she had worn all day and went to the closet to choose one to wear for the evening.

She chose a long one, black, white and green printed cotton with a full wide skirt edged with a frill and a sleeveless top which plunged to a deep revealing V both at the front and the back.

Wearing high-heeled strapped sandals and wondering why she had dressed up, she went slowly downstairs. Voices speaking excitedly in Portuguese were coming from the direction of the *sala*—men's voices which sounded familiar. Her heart thumping with anticipation, Delia went towards the room and walked straight into Rita, her face flushed and her eyes shining, who was coming out in a rush.

'Ah, I was coming for you. See who is here!' she cried excitedly, and gestured to the two men who were standing in the middle of the *sala* drinking from tall glasses. Manoel and Carlo.

'Where is Edmund?' asked Delia.

'Ah, Delia, it is good to see you.' Carlo set down his glass and came straight to her to gather her into his arms and give her the *abraço*. 'How I wish you weren't married to that cold, tough devil of a doctor,' he said teasingly, smiling down at her. 'I would like very much to marry you myself.' His face grew serious. 'The truth is we do not know now where he is. We thought he would be here with you. He and Zanetta left us on Wednesday morning to fly to Brasilia and catch a plane for here. He was anxious for some reason to be in Rio before Wednesday evening. We cannot think what might have happened. Even if he could not get a plane at Brasilia which would have brought him on Wednesday he should have arrived here yesterday.'

'Did anyone come yesterday while we were away?' Delia asked Rita, her throat suddenly dry and her hands clammy with fear.

'I have asked Dulva. She says no one came and there was only one phone call, for you.'

'For me? Then it must have been from Edmund.'

'No,' Rita shook her head. 'It was a woman. She asked if you were here and hung up while Dulva was telling her that you had gone away for two days.'

'But I don't know any woman in Rio apart from you,' cried Delia.

'Could it have been someone calling from the airline about your reservation?' suggested Manoel.

'Surely someone like that would have left a message,' mused Carlo, who was frowning thoughtfully. 'Did the woman speak in English or Portuguese?'

'Portuguese. How else would Dulva understand her?' retorted Rita.

'With a foreign accent?' persisted Carlo.

'How do I know?' Rita made a gesture of helplessness.

'Ask Dulva,' said Carlo. 'If there was no foreign accent, if the woman was Brazilian and from Rio, it's my guess that she was Zanetta.'

'Zanetta?' They all stared at him as if he were crazy.

'*Sim*,' he replied, nodding at them, his dark eyes very bright. 'She is very tricky, that one, very tricky. I suggest that we phone her home to find out if she is back. She and Edmund left Fenenal together, so maybe they are still together. Ah, forgive me, Delia,' he added quickly as he saw her flinch and go pale. 'I speak my mind without thinking. I'm sure everything will be all right and that there is perfectly good reason why Edmund didn't come here. We have to find out somehow where he has gone, so I suggest we start with Zanetta.'

'Then I will go at once and phone her,' said Rita. 'Manoel, please make Delia a drink. She is a little upset, I think.'

'I'll come with you to the phone,' said Carlo suddenly, striding after Rita. 'If you don't have any luck with Zanetta I might.'

Sitting on the edge of one of the armchairs in the *sala*, Delia sipped the drink Manoel had made for her and tried to listen to all he was telling her about the 'flu epidemic on Fenenal. But the words slid past her ears. All she could think of was that Edmund had travelled with Zanetta on Wednesday and had not arrived, and that could mean that he had gone away somewhere with the Brazilian woman.

Rita and Carlo came back into the room. Carlo was muttering in Portuguese and Rita was looking very worried. Delia sprang to her feet.

'Did you speak to Zanetta? Was she there? Oh, tell me, what did she say?'

'Yes, she was there,' sighed Rita, sinking down in a chair and taking the glass Manoel handed to her. 'She doesn't know where Edmund is. She hasn't seen him since yesterday morning. It seems they were unable to fly to Rio from Brasilia on Wednesday because the plane they should have taken was grounded due to engine trouble. They came on Thursday morning as soon as they could.'

'And was it she who phoned here asking for Delia?' asked Manoel.

'*Sim*,' Rita nodded. 'She said she offered to phone for Edmund. He had tried twice and couldn't get through. He wanted to know if Delia was here . . .'

'And she told him all she thought he should know,' put in Carlo viciously. 'That Delia had gone away.'

'He would think I'd gone to England on Wednesday,' said Delia woodenly. 'He would think I hadn't waited for him.'

'Zanetta said she invited him to go to her home to stay there, but he refused. She says he just walked away from her and she hasn't seen him since,' said Rita. 'Where do you think he would go? What would he do?'

'Find out how soon he could fly to England too,' said Manoel simply. 'That's what I would do. He could be in London now if there was a flight out yesterday.'

'And if he could get on it,' said Carlo.

'Well, how do we find out?' asked Delia, looking at each of them in turn.

'We phone all the international airlines having either direct flights to Britain or connecting flights. There are several ways he could have gone, via New York or via Georgetown,' said Carlo. 'No, we won't do that, we'll go to the airport to find out. Some of them won't give out information about passengers over the phone. If you will lend me a car I'll drive Delia out there now. Will you come?' he asked Delia.

'Yes, yes, of course.' She glanced at her watch. 'There's a flight due to take off in about three-quarters of an hour, the same one I should have taken on Wednesday. If he wasn't able to get on a flight yesterday he might be going on that.'

'Then we must hurry,' said Carlo.

They went in Maria's green Volkswagen. Sitting tensely beside Carlo, Delia stared out at the heaving mass of dark ocean as they drove along the narrow avenue which led to the city.

'Why do you think Zanetta did what she did?' she asked.

'Women in love, women who are jealous, do strange things,' said Carlo lightly. 'She's in love with Edmund and jealous of you and she found herself suddenly with a card to play. She knew he was anxious to reach Rio before you left for England and so she thought that if she could show him you had left before he arrived, that you hadn't cared enough to wait for him, she might be able to part him from you once and for all. You see, he had been saying before you turned up at Posto Orlando that he might stay in Brazil. She took a chance, but it didn't come off. He walked away from her. That should prove something to you.'

'What?'

'That he isn't in love with her,' said Carlo dryly.

'I suppose so,' Delia sighed.

The traffic was heavy going into the city and as they swept round a wide square Delia noticed that the stands had been erected where people would sit to watch the Carnival parades go by. Round the beautiful Praça Paris they drove on to the Avenida Atlantica beside Copacabana beach. People sat on benches either watching the traffic go by or turned the other way to watch the glittering surf. Here and there on the sand light glowed where candles had been lit and placed in little hollows as part of the voodoo ritual of *macumba*.

Although Carlo drove fast it was almost time for the take-off of the plane bound for London when they arrived at the international airport at Galeao. Carlo let Delia off at the entrance to the departure lounge and drove away to park the car. Dashing through the doorway, Delia went straight to the desk of the British airline to ask if Edmund was booked on the flight which was taking off, explaining that she was his wife. The ticket agent looked through the list of passengers and shook his head.

'Could he have gone yesterday?' she asked.

'Not with us,' he replied, and told her the names of two other airlines with which Edmund could have flown direct to London on the previous day.

To her relief Carlo appeared and together they went to the desk of the other airlines. It took a while and a certain amount of bullying on the part of Carlo, but at last they found out that Edmund had boarded a plane flying to London on Thursday evening.

Delia sagged with dismay.

'Oh, what shall I do now?' she exclaimed.

'You could stay and watch the Carnival with me,' suggested Carlo with a smile. 'But I think it would be best if you find out now how soon you can fly to England too.'

CHAPTER SEVEN

DELIA left Rio the day the Carnival parades began, and as she was driven to Galeao airport she had a glimpse of the groups of colourful dancing, singing people winding their way through the streets of the city to the rhythmic beats of the *sambas* and the *bossa-novas* specially composed for the occasion.

Her leavetaking from her newly-found Brazilian friends was very Brazilian, a mixture of tears and laughter and many *abraços*. The flight was long and tedious above the dark waters of the ocean and she didn't sleep much.

The weather was cold and wet at Heathrow and the airport lounges were crowded as usual with people waiting to board planes or waiting to meet arrivals. But there was no one to meet her.

Biting her lip to keep back the tears of disappointment and tiredness which welled in her eyes, Delia found an empty telephone kiosk and searched through the directory for Ben Davies's home number. She had half-expected Edmund to meet her off the plane. She had hoped that Ben, to whom she had sent a cable saying when she hoped to be back, had been able to contact Edmund in some way and alert him. But it seemed as if that hadn't happened. Either Ben had not been able to find Edmund or if he had Edmund had decided he didn't want to meet her.

Ben answered the phone almost immediately.

'So you're back. About time too,' he growled. 'How are you?'

'A little tired after that flight. Did you get my cable?'

'Yes, I did. What the hell are you and Edmund playing at?' he queried.

'We're not playing at anything. We missed each other in Rio through a misunderstanding and I don't know where he is any more. Didn't he phone you to find out if I was back?'

'No, he didn't. But I know that he's arrived in England. I phoned O.S.P.P. as soon as I received your cable yesterday morning and they said he'd been in to see them on Friday afternoon just after flying in from Rio. He left them saying he'd let them have his report as soon as he'd finished it.'

'Didn't he tell them where he was going?' asked Delia.

'Yes, for once he did. He said he was going to attend to some family business. Hang on a minute—I have the name of the place right here.' There was a clattering sound as Ben put down the receiver. He was back in a few seconds. 'This is it. Chance Court, Hampshire. Mean anything to you?'

'Yes, oh yes, that's where his great-uncle, Justin Talbot, lives. I'll go there right away.'

'Now, hang on a minute, girl,' put in Ben. 'Have you any idea exactly where in Hampshire it is?'

'It's between Winchester and Salisbury, Wiltshire. Near a place called Middle Dene.'

'Hmm. I thought so, down in the deep south, you might say, miles away from anywhere. How were you thinking of getting there?' asked the ever-practical Ben.

'Well, I suppose I could take a train to Winchester and then a bus from there to Middle Dene?'

'On a Sunday, in the winter?' Ben sounded scornful. 'I doubt if there are any buses going to a place like that today. You'd be better off going by car. Look, why don't you stay where you are and I'll come and pick you up? You can come here for a bite of Sunday dinner. We're having roast beef and

Yorkshire pud. We're in the right direction for Winchester and you can borrow Audrey's car. You could even phone ahead from here to make sure Edmund's at Chance Court before you set off.'

The offer of dinner and a car made her feel much better. She agreed. Going to Ben's house, taking his advice was preferable to doing everything on her own when she felt so tired and dispirited, and she settled down with a cup of coffee in a restaurant to await his arrival.

He came about three-quarters of an hour later and they went out to the car park where Ben's Yorkshire terrier Pinch was sitting on the back seat of his car looking very mournful.

'Before I came out I looked up Chance Court and found the best way for you to go there,' said Ben as they drove out along the road to Windsor. In the distance the round tower of the castle looked dour and brooding in the grey light of the wet day, and staring out at the winter-bleached grass and the leafless trees Delia found it hard to realise that she was in the same world in which Posto Orlando and Binauros existed. The hot blue skies, the thick luxuriant growth of the jungle, the steamy atmosphere seemed like a fantastic dream.

'It's one of the stately homes of England. Gardens and some public rooms open to the public in the summer,' Ben went on. 'Did you know that?'

'No, Edmund never talked about it.'

'Funny lad, Edmund,' growled Ben. 'Very secretive, if you ask me. How did you and he get on in the jungle?'

'I thought we were getting on all right until I told him about losing the baby.'

'Took it badly, did he?'

'Very badly,' she whispered.

Ben and his wife lived in a renovated eighteenth-century cottage close to an old square-towered Norman church in a tiny village near Ascot. Audrey met them at the door.

'Ooh, what a lovely tan you have, Delia!' she exclaimed. 'I bet you wish you could have stayed in Brazil. We've been having miserable weather here. Would you like a glass of sherry before you eat?'

Dinner as usual was excellent and Delia ate as if she had been starving for months. Afterwards she found the telephone number of Chance Court with the help of Directory Inquiries. A man answered the phone. He spoke coolly and a little stiffly and told her that Dr Talbot was staying at the Court but was out for the afternoon. Could he take a message?

'Just tell him when he returns that Delia called,' she replied breathlessly. She put down the receiver and turned to Ben. 'He's staying there,' she said, her eyes shining.

'That's fine. It isn't far, but it'll take you a good two and a half hours to get there and since it's nearly three o'clock now you best set off if you want to arrive before it goes dark,' Ben suggested.

Audrey's car was a small Austin. She explained its peculiarities to Delia and then stood back to wave goodbye as Delia backed it out into the road. Ben had a last word through the car window.

'Come back here if you're not invited to stay for the night,' he said with a cheeky grin. 'And take it easy. The roads are slippery.'

In spite of his warnings she drove as fast as the speed limit on the road to Winchester would let her. There wasn't much traffic because of the wet day and after an hour's driving she reached a roundabout where there was a signpost indicating that the road to Storton was to the right.

It was a narrow road and it seemed to wander about aimlessly. It climbed ridges and dipped down into valleys. It passed through small villages of thatched-roofed cottages and skirted round wide fields where clumps of trees raised bare branches to the lowering grey clouds. Sometimes it was enclosed by high hawthorn hedges and sometimes it was edged by stone walls over which she could see the land rolling away into a murky distance.

It went on for miles and miles and as she turned each bend Delia hoped to see a cluster of houses and a couple of church towers which would indicate that she had arrived at Storton.

Tiredness, the result of the long flight from Brazil to Britain, was beginning to nag at her nerves and make her eyes ache, and when she at last reached Storton she was glad to park the car in the wide main street outside the porticoed entrance to the hotel which had once been an old coaching inn.

She was served afternoon tea in a pretty chintzy dining room and was told by the pleasant friendly woman who served her that it was only ten miles to Middle Dene and that Chance Court was five miles beyond the village.

The ten miles along another even narrower, more twisting lane seemed to take forever, and lights were glowing from windows in the tiny village of Middle Dene. Delia drove straight through as instructed by the woman in the hotel at Storton and went along slowly looking for a turning to the left. It appeared at last. There was a signpost at the corner with the name Chance Court on it and, her spirits lifting, she turned into the lane. Now all she had to do was look out for a fork in the road.

The rain which had held off for a while came down heavily so that she felt she was driving through a thick grey haze. She switched on the headlights and drove a little faster and was past the fork in the road before she realised, going along the wrong lane, the one to the left instead of the one to the right.

Braking, she changed into reverse gear, backed up, misjudged the closeness of the wheels of the car to the grassy verge and felt the car tip sideways as one of its rear wheels sank into a ditch. At once she braked and changed gear again. The engine roared, the rear wheel which was sunk in the mud spun round, but the car didn't move. No matter what she did it stayed right where it was, stuck in the mud. She would have to walk the rest of the way to Chance Court.

Tying her scarf over her head to protect it from the rain, she scrambled out of the car, locked its doors and tightening the belt of her trench coat walked back to the place where the road forked and where a signpost informed her that she was on her way to Chance Court, once the home of the Chance family.

She walked beside a stone wall which was green with moss and overhung with hawthorns and wild rose bushes. The ditch between her and the wall was full of water gushing along noisily. Behind her she could hear the sound of a car approaching, the swish of tyres on a wet surface, the muted roar of an expensive engine.

She stepped on to the grass verge. The car passed her and she was sprayed with mud churned up by its wheels. It came to a sudden skidding stop. Its stopping lights blinked angrily, then it began to come backwards, the reversing lights coming on instead of the stopping lights.

It stopped beside her. The nearside window was rolled down and a voice, a dearly-loved familiar voice spoke from within.

'Are you going to the Court? Can I give you a lift?'

Her heart beating wildly, Delia stepped forward and bent a little to peer in through the open window at the driver of the car and saw his blue eyes go wide in shocked surprise.

'Yes, Edmund, I'd like a lift, please. I'm going to the Court to see you,' she said, and he continued to stare at her

in amazement. 'It's really me—Delia,' she added frantically.
'Oh, unlock the door, Edmund, and let me in! I'm getting
awfully wet standing out here.'

He leaned across and pulled back the lever to unlock the
door. She pulled it open and slid into the seat beside him.
The inside of the car was warm and soft music was coming
from the radio. Taking off her wet scarf, she shook out her
flattened hair and turned to him, smiling a little hesitantly.
One elbow rested on the steering wheel as he supported his
head on his hand, still staring at her as if he couldn't believe
his eyes.

'How did you get here?' he said at last in a croaky voice as
if his throat was dry.

'By car. It's in the ditch on the other road,' she said. How
different he looked from the last time she had seen him.
Over an open-necked shirt and thin V-necked woollen
sweater he was wearing a dark grey suede jacket which
matched in colour his trousers of fine worsted wool. His hair
had been cut and although it wasn't very short it wasn't
tangled, and the change in style made him look older, more
severe and remote.

He switched off the radio but left the windscreen wipers
and the engine going and looked at her again. Now that he
was over the surprise his glance was more critical, a little
cold.

'I don't want to appear too curious,' he said softly, 'but
would you mind telling me where you've been since you left
Posto Orlando?'

'I went to Rio with Rita as arranged. I stayed with her at
her parents' house,' she replied, a little surprised by the
question.

'You weren't there last Thursday,' he said tautly, and put
the car into gear so that it began to move forward slowly.

'I know,' she said nervously, biting her lip and glancing away out of the window beside her. This meeting wasn't as she had planned it. He wasn't pleased to see her. 'Rita and I went to Petropolis.'

'Where the hell is that?' he growled.

'In the hills, behind Rio.'

'But you left Rio last Wednesday,' he said, flicking her a cold glance.

'No, I didn't. I waited for you to come and you didn't come,' she explained.

'Couldn't you have waited a little longer?' he asked dryly.

'It was so hot and Rita suggested we should go for the day to see Manoel's parents. If you have any idea what waiting for someone is like you know that you're glad to fill in the time doing anything to take your mind off the possibility that the person you're waiting for might not come.' Her voice wavered, she swallowed and added more strongly, 'We left a message with the housekeeper to tell you and Manoel if you turned up or phoned that we would be back and that *you* were to wait for *us*.'

He was silent. The car's engine purred softly and the windscreen wipers swished back and forth, sweeping away the grew rain. The long stone wall came to an end at a wide gateway guarded by big stone gateposts on which a coat of arms was carved. The car slowed down and turned in between the gateposts, gathered speed again and swept up a long winding dark grey driveway between two rows of oak trees towards an elegant stone house which stood on a hill overlooking sweeping lawns.

'What a lovely place!' exclaimed Delia, but Edmund didn't answer her but drove past the house into a courtyard, bringing the car to a stop in front of a stable which had been converted into garages. He switched everything off and gave her a hard unsmiling glance.

'Now that you're here, you'd better come in and do some explaining,' he said.

'Thank you,' she said, and turned away quickly to open the car door so that he wouldn't see the sudden trembling of her mouth.

They walked through the drizzle to the front of the house and mounted the shallow steps to the front door. It opened slowly and a man appeared. He was tall, had thinning grey hair and looked very stern. He was dressed in a dark suit and a white shirt with a black tie.

'Good evening, sir,' he said, and sent a curious glance in Delia's direction.

'Good evening, Jonas,' said Edmund, and putting a hand under Delia's elbow urged her through the door and into a wide high entrance hall with a gleaming polished floor and an ornately-plastered ceiling.

'A young woman phoned, Dr Talbot. She wouldn't leave a message, just said to tell you Delia called,' said the man.

'This is she,' said Edmund, his voice softening a little with amusement. 'My wife. Jonas is the butler here, Delia, and has been with my Uncle Justin for nearly thirty years.'

'I'm pleased to meet you, madam,' said the butler coolly. 'May I take your raincoat?'

'Thank you,' said Delia, untying the belt. Jonas moved behind her and lifted the raincoat from her shoulders.

'Would you like some tea, madam?' he asked, placing the coat over his arm.

'Yes, please.'

'In the drawing room?'

'Would ... would that be all right?' asked Delia nervously, finding his cold severe manner intimidating.

'No, it wouldn't,' said Edmund brusquely. 'I'd prefer to have it in the breakfast room. I hope you've kept the fire going in there, Jonas, as I told you. *Brrr*, this place is like a morgue!'

The butler tried not to seem offended, but didn't really succeed, and with a brief nod at Delia he marched off down the hallway with her coat.

'I think you've hurt his feelings,' Delia whispered to Edmund.

'I don't really care if I have,' he retorted. 'He doesn't like me and he never has. I don't fit in with his ideas on how a descendant of the Chance family should behave. Come on, let's go and sit by that fire. You must be feeling the cold as much as I am, having just come back from the tropics.'

She followed him across the shining oak floor to a half-open door and they entered a pleasant room panelled in oak and furnished with an oval table and spindle-backed windsor chairs. A fire of smokeless fuel flickered in the fireplace, a cheerful welcoming glow in the fast-dimming light of the wet February evening. Edmund pulled up a cushioned rocking chair to the hearth and suggested she sat down. He squatted down before the fire and held out his hands to it to warm them.

'Are you really a descendant of the Chance family?' she asked.

'Yes. My great-grandmother was a Chance. She was the last of the line. Her father died impoverished, leaving her this place. She married Mortimer Talbot, toffee maker—for his money, of course,' he said dryly, flicking her a sardonic glance. 'It was something which seems to happen regularly to Talbot men. She used his ill-gotten gains to preserve this place. When she died she left it to her younger son Justin, who seemed to be the only one interested in the place, and unless I can do something very quickly he's going to leave it to me in his will.' His mouth curved in a mirthless smile. 'Ironic, isn't it, that I who want so little in the way of possessions and money should gather so much.'

'Hasn't he any children or grandchildren he could leave it to?' asked Delia.

'No, he never married. But he always had a soft spot for me ever since my father brought me to visit here when I was a boy.' He stared at the flames of the fire, his expression morose. 'Poor old Justin,' he said softly. 'He's in hospital now, in intensive care. That's where I've been this afternoon. I doubt if he'll survive the stroke. The message that he was ill was waiting for me at O.S.P.P. headquarters when I called in there on Friday.'

'I'm sorry he's ill,' Delia said quietly, and also stared at the fire as the gloom deepened in the room. Edmund reached and pulled a low stool from the corner beside the fireplace and without straightening up pushed it beneath him so that he was sitting on it still in front of the fire.

'How did you find out I was here?' he asked.

'Ben told me and he found out from O.S.P.P. when he received my cable asking him to find out where you were. He told me this morning when I arrived back from Brazil. Edmund, why did you let Zanetta do your phoning for you? Why didn't you phone Rita's home yourself?'

He glanced at her sharply. In the firelight his face had a ruddy glow which made his eyes seem more blue.

'I did. I spoke to the housekeeper twice.' He grinned suddenly and ruefully. 'To say the least of it, we had problems with communicating. I couldn't understand her accent, so in the end Zanetta offered to phone for me. All she said was that you'd gone away and that Rita wasn't there either, and I thought you'd . . .' he broke off and shaded his face with one hand. 'God, I don't know what I thought,' he muttered. 'I'd tried hard to reach Rio before you were due to leave, but there were so many damned silly delays on the way, and to hear that you had gone away only confirmed what I'd been expecting anyway.'

'You mean you didn't expect me to wait for you?' she exclaimed.

'I hoped you would wait, but I didn't expect you would,' he replied. He stared at the fire, his face set in bitter lines. 'I walked off and left Zanetta standing there.' He laughed shortly. 'God knows what she must have thought, but it doesn't matter any more. What I don't understand is why didn't the housekeeper give Zanetta the whole of the message which you and Rita had left?'

'She was going to, but as soon as she had said I'd gone away Zanetta hung up, didn't wait.'

Edmund stared at her with puzzlement shadowing his eyes.

'Why?' he demanded. 'Why would she do something like that?' Before she could answer there was a knock on the door of the room and it opened slowly. Jonas stepped in, flicked on the light switch so that two floor lamps came on to cast a rosy glow over the dark panelling. Stepping across the room, he pulled the heavy draperies across the window.

He was followed by a tall thin woman in a black dress who was carrying a big tray on which silver and china glinted. She set the tray down on the table and stood with her hands folded on her stomach to stare curiously with bright eyes at Delia.

With an expression of resignation on his face Edmund rose to his feet and stood with his back to the fire.

'This is my uncle's housekeeper, Mrs Mills,' he drawled. 'Mrs Mills, I'd like you to meet my wife.'

'Welcome to Chance Court, Mrs Talbot,' said the woman in a soft burring country accent. Her face creased into a warm smile which made up for Jonas's frozen looks. 'I've made some sandwiches and there's a dish of trifle and some fruit cake. I expect you're hungry after your journey down here. Would you like a fire lit in the bedroom, Dr Talbot?'

'Is that possible?' asked Edmund in surprise.

'Oh yes.'

'Then I'd appreciate it very much,' he said. 'Jonas, perhaps you'd find a way of rescuing the car which Mrs Talbot came in out of the ditch on the Fallowdene road and bringing it here. What sort of a car is it, Delia?'

'A yellow Austin. It isn't very far along. Here are the keys.'

'Thank you, madam.' Jonas took the keys from her. 'Is that all, sir?'

'That's all, except that Mrs Talbot and I would like to have our tea without any further interruptions. Is that clear?' said Edmund coldly.

'Quite clear, sir.'

The butler and the housekeeper withdrew and closed the door. Delia got to her feet and went to pour tea from the heavy ornate silver teapot into thin china cups.

'And Jonas thinks you don't know how to behave like a Chance,' she teased, handing a cup of tea to Edmund, who had just sat down in the rocking chair leaving the stool for her. 'It seems to me you did a very good imitation of someone who might be lord and master of this house just now.'

'If I didn't speak to him like that he'd start ordering me about in the way he's ordered old Justin about for the past thirty years,' he retorted. 'And he's so damned nosy. Has to know everything. He'll be back, you'll see, on some excuse or other, just to see what you and I are doing.' He let his breath out in a sharp, short sigh. 'What the hell am I going to do with the place if Uncle dies and I inherit it? I don't want it.'

'You could live in it, or at least in part of it, like your uncle has,' Delia suggested, and bit into a sandwich. It was wafer-thin and filled with some sort of shrimp mixture. It was delicious and went in two bites. She helped herself to another and passed the plate to Edmund, who took a handful of them.

'Imagine me living in a place like this,' he scoffed. 'It's too big. Even if . . .' He broke off, scowled and began to eat the sandwiches.

'Even if what?' Delia prompted.

'Doesn't matter,' he muttered. 'Why do you think Zanetta hung up before the housekeeper finished giving her the message?'

'She told Rita that she'd thought that was all there was to know. But Carlo believes she did it deliberately.'

'Carlo?' he queried, giving her a hard look over the rim of his teacup. 'So he was there too, was he? Did he say why he believed that?'

'Yes.' Delia stared into the flames of the fire. 'Zanetta was being like Peter. She was jealous of me in the same way Peter was jealous of you. She wanted to come between us. She knew you were hoping I'd still be in Rio and she tried to make you think I didn't care enough about you to wait. She hoped you would stay in Brazil with her.' Delia paused and since he didn't say anything asked, 'Would you like some trifle or fruit cake?'

'Trifle,' he muttered absently. 'But I'll get it.' He went over to the table and behind her she could hear the clink of a spoon against glass dishes as he served the trifle. He came back, thrust a full dish at her and sat down in the chair again to stare at the dish he was holding for himself. He shook his head slowly from side to side as if puzzled.

'I don't know where Zanetta got the idea that I was interested in her,' he said suddenly. 'If I ever thought of her at all it was as a doctor, and not a very good one at that. She had no real concern for the people she was supposed to be healing and she was a dead loss at Fenenal.'

'She told me that she'd only gone as a volunteer because she wanted to be near you after she'd met you. And she did save your life.'

'Did she tell you that?' He was both amused and amazed. 'What a lot of nonsense! I'd have survived without her hovering around me bathing my brow every few minutes and taking my temperature,' he added scornfully. 'She was a damned nuisance. I had to tell her to clear out so I could sleep.' He shrugged. 'What the hell! I was fool enough to believe what she said, that you'd gone away.'

'In the same way you believed Peter,' Delia muttered miserably. 'Where did you go when you walked away from her?'

'Walked about in circles as if I were punch-drunk,' he replied self-mockingly, 'and then went by taxi to Galeao airport to see if I could fly to England that day. I was lucky and when I reached London I went straight to the flat. One look at the dust on the furniture and I knew you weren't there and hadn't been there for some time. I went to O.S.P.P., then tried the flat again later without any luck. Then I phoned Ben at his office. I was too late, the place had closed for the week-end. I had no idea where he lived, so I gave up and drove down here.' He stood up and went to put his empty dish on the table. 'More trifle or tea?' he asked politely.

'No, thank you.' She stood up too and went to put her

dishes on the tray. 'Why did you want to find me?' she asked tentatively.

'To ask you why you hadn't waited for me,' he replied coolly.

'Oh, if only you'd trusted me, none of this would have happened,' she cried out, suddenly tired of the way they were dodging round the real issue. 'If you'd taken a taxi to Rita's home instead of to the international airport you'd have found out I'd waited for you. But you trusted Zanetta more than you trusted me. You trusted Peter more than you trusted me.' She swallowed, searching for the courage to say something which had to be said. 'I don't believe you love me,' she accused in a low voice. 'If you loved me you'd trust me . . . oh, Edmund, please don't look like that! What are you going to do?'

His hands had shot out and were about her throat and he was glaring down at her, his eyes bright and hard.

'You might well look frightened, darling,' he said between set teeth. 'I'm pretty close to wringing your neck!'

'Why? What have I done?'

'Something you're always doing, accusing me of not loving you,' he said softly, stingingly, his hands relaxing but staying where they were, the finger tips moving slightly suggestively on the skin of her throat. 'I married you because I love you. I left you because I loved you, because I couldn't bear the thought of you being unhappy married to me, to give you a chance to divorce me. I went away, far away, cut all connection hoping to get you out of my system. I thought I'd succeeded. I thought I was self-contained again when you turned up at Posto Orlando and although I tried to keep you out, you began to take over again, to separate me from sanity . . .'

'Ahem!' The cough was loud enough to make them both

look round in surprise. Jonas was standing just inside the
door of the room, and Edmund sighed with exasperation.
His hands fell away from Delia's throat and he thrust them
into his trouser pockets.

'I thought I told you we weren't to be interrupted,' he
grated. 'What is it now?'

'Mrs Talbot's car, sir. Price, Mr Justin's chauffeur, has
managed to pull it out of the ditch and it is now parked in
the stableyard.

'Thank you, Jonas,' said Delia.

'Not at all, madam. I hope everything is all right,
madam?'

'Yes, thank you.' Delia smiled at him and to her surprise
he smiled back—if you could call the faint movement of his
severe mouth a smile.

'Is that all, sir?'

'Yes, that's all, Jonas.' Again Edmund sounded as if he
were talking through set teeth. 'You may go. And don't
come back.'

'Very well, sir.'

He picked up the tea tray and went off towards the door.
There he turned and said stiffly,

'The fire is lit in the bedroom now. It should be warming
up nicely.'

He walked out, leaving the door slightly open. They
waited until the sound of his footsteps had faded, then
looked at each other again. The blaze had faded from Edmund's eyes. They were dark and sombre as their glance
went to her throat.

'Oh God, I've hurt you again,' he groaned, touching her
throat with gentle fingers. 'Yet I love you and only you.
That's why I left Fenenal before I should have done, to try
and be in Rio before you left. That's why I followed you, or

thought I'd followed you to London as soon as I could. That's why I don't want you to come to the jungle or any of those other places where I have to go in case you catch a fever and die. I love you. You're inside me here.' He touched his head. 'And I can't get rid of you. I've been going through hell these past few days wondering where you were, wondering if I'd lost you again because I was so bloody-minded about the baby. That's why I behave crazily when I see you with another man ... God, Delia, what else do I have to say to convince you?'

'Nothing, nothing, nothing—I'm convinced!' She was laughing and crying at the same time. 'Oh, Edmund, I love you too, that's why I want to be where you are always. Please can I stay the night here with you? Please!'

Her hands were on his arms, her face was lifted in appeal.

'I wasn't thinking of letting you stay the night anywhere else,' he murmured, framing her face with his hands. 'So shall we start all over again?' he asked.

'I thought we had, in a hammock in the jungle,' she whispered.

'On our second honeymoon,' he added, his eyes gleaming with tender laughter as he bent his head to kiss her. Their lips met tentatively. His arms went around her and suddenly passion flared and their bodies swayed with the intensity of their feelings as they clung to each other, oblivious to the knock on the door and the quiet swish of it being pushed open.

'Ahem, excuse me, sir.' At the sound of the cool incisive voice they broke apart and turned to stare at Jonas.

'What's the matter now?' demanded Edmund roughly.

'We ... that is, Price and I ... were wondering if Mrs Talbot will be needing her car again tonight. If not Price will put it away in the garage with yours, sir, if he may have your keys. It's a very damp night and it won't do the cars any good at all to stand out in the rain.'

'Here.' Edmund tossed his keys across the room, and looking very affronted Jonas caught them. 'Mrs Talbot is staying the night and will stay here as long as I have to,' added Edmund crisply. 'Now is that all, Jonas?'

'Yes, sir. I think so, sir.'

'Then goodnight.'

'Goodnight, sir, madam.'

He went away. Edmund grabbed Delia's hand and pulling her after him went out into the hall too.

'Where are we going?' she asked as he made for the elegant curving staircase.

'To bed. It's the only place I can think of where we can talk without any further interruptions. At least I think we can. I think there's a lock and key on the door.'

The bedroom was wide and lofty, lit by glowing, dancing firelight which glinted on the triple mirror of the dressing table and on the brass rods of the bed ends. Edmund flicked a switch and the bedside lamps came on.

'What a huge bed!' exclaimed Delia.

'Sleeps about six,' replied Edmund, taking off his suede jacket and throwing it across a chair. 'A bit different from a hammock in the jungle with the drums beating outside the hut!'

'I haven't any nightclothes with me,' said Delia, hugging herself with her arms. Even in her woollen pant suit and rolled-neck sweater she could feel the cold seeping into her. Only near the fire was it warm.

'I haven't any either,' said Edmund. 'I had time only to buy the clothes I'm wearing on Friday.' He stripped off the V-necked sweater and his shirt and began to take off his trousers. 'The idea is to undress as fast as you can and leap into bed and huddle under the blankets. I'll get in first and warm the sheets for you.'

In the middle of the big bed they lay entwined, not making love, content to be there close together in the fire-glow.

'I'm still finding it hard to believe we're together again,' Edmund murmured.

'How long do you think we'll stay at the Court?' she asked.

'I don't know. It depends on what happens to Uncle Justin. We'll talk about it tomorrow. Right now I can think of more important things to do.' His mouth hovered close to hers. 'There's just one thing, Delia, before we go any further. Do you want to have another baby?'

'Would you like to have one?' she countered. 'If we had another would it help you to forgive me for losing the first one?'

He groaned and buried his face against her shoulder.

'There was nothing to forgive,' he whispered. 'It wasn't the loss of the baby that made me lash out at you. It was being left out of something which was important to both of us. Afterwards I realised you'd had to suffer much more. You'd had to go through it alone. I won't let you go through that again by yourself.'

'But supposing you go away again? I know you've been asked to work for the protection service in Brazil at Posto Orlando,' she whispered.

'I haven't decided yet,' he replied. 'And if there's the slightest chance of you becoming pregnant I'm not going anywhere that will take me far away from you until the child is born. But we'll talk about it tomorrow.'

'Tomorrow, tomorrow,' she repeated teasingly. 'How Brazilian you've become!'

'Perhaps,' he smiled. 'Or perhaps I've learned at last to put first things first. Mmm, you smell of sandalwood and your skin is smooth and soft and you don't seem to have any bones,' he said softly. 'Tell me, darling, have you always gone limp and quivery when I've kissed you—like this—or when I've touched you—like this?'

'Always,' she moaned ecstatically, pressing herself close against his hard warm body.

'Then I think you should know that it has the most devastating effect on me,' he murmured, his mouth against the soft swell of her breasts.

This was the Edmund she had fallen in love with, gently mocking yet exquisitely considerate of her needs. But now she knew that there was much more to him than the tender coaxing lover and that loving him meant accepting the whole man.

'Oh, Edmund, I do love you,' she whispered. The feeling seemed to well up and overflow.

'Even though I've hurt you and might hurt you again?'

'I've hurt you too,' she said, twisting her fingers in his hair. 'It's all been a part of learning to love.'

'I've been thinking along the same lines myself,' he jeered gently, and she felt his breath feather across her mouth, then his lips were against hers, hard and possessive, and she lost all sense of time and place. She knew only the quick urgent demand of his body pressing against hers and the quick leaping of her own desire before their minds and bodies fused in perfect union.

And afterwards there was silence as they slept in each other's arms in the middle of the huge bed while the fire died down slowly and the room became dark.

Best Seller Romances

Next month's best loved romances

Mills & Boon Best Seller Romances are the love stories that have proved particularly popular with our readers. These are the titles to look out for next month.

BEWILDERED HAVEN Helen Bianchin
THE MATCHMAKERS Janet Dailey
MASTER OF COMUS Charlotte Lamb
THE MARQUIS TAKES A WIFE Rachel Lindsay
LOREN'S BABY Anne Mather
REEDS OF HONEY Margaret Way

HAWK IN A BLUE SKY
by Charlotte Lamb

was five years since Amanda had turned down Cesare's proposal
marriage, but now she was going back again to his home in
scany – this time engaged to his younger brother Piero. And it
n became clear that Cesare was not going to accept the new
ation any more than he had accepted the old. But what could
nanda do about it?

THE WRONG MAN TO LOVE
by Roberta Leigh

mantha supposed her beloved godfather had known what he
s doing when he left her the controlling shares in his huge
partment store – but how she wished he hadn't done it! For all it
to was her falling in love with Zachary Farrell, the new head of
business – who naturally had no time for her at all!

LORD OF LA PAMPA
by Kay Thorpe

en Lian was stranded in Buenos Aires Ricardo Mendoza
cued her from a very dangerous predicament – and thereby put
in his debt. But it seemed there was a way she could repay him –
becoming his wife, in name only, for the next six months. It
med little enough to commit herself to in the circumstances,
. . .

THE LOVED AND THE FEARED
by Violet Winspear

e world-famous film star Serafina Neri made slaves of the men
surrounded her – even her spoilt son Adone – so what was
ng Donna Lovelace to do when she fell in love with Rick
detti, who seemed to be at Serafina's beck and call day
night?

the rose of romance

How to join in a whole new world of romance

It's very easy to subscribe to the Mills & Boon Reader Service. As a regular reader, you can enjoy a whole range of special benefits. Bargain offers. Big cash savings. Your own free Reader Service newsletter, packed with knitting patterns, recipes, competitions, and exclusive book offers.

We send you the very latest titles each month, postage and packing free – no hidden extra charges. There's absolutely no commitment – you receive books for only as long as you want.

We'll send you details. Simply send the coupon – or drop us a line for details about the Mills & Boon Reader Service Subscription Scheme. Post to: Mills & Boon Reader Service, P.O. Box 236, Thornton Road, Croydon, Surrey CR9 3RU, England. *Please note: READERS IN SOUTH AFRICA please write to: Mills & Boon Reader Service of Southern Africa, Private Bag X3010, Randburg 2125, S. Africa.

Please send me details of the Mills & Boon Subscription Scheme.

NAME (Mrs/Miss) _____ EP3

ADDRESS _____

_____

COUNTY/COUNTRY _____ POST/ZIP CODE _____

BLOCK LETTERS, PLEASE

Mills & Boon
the rose of romance